A Gift from Crick

Sailors Diggings, an isolated mining settlement, is left reeling when outlaws slaughter seventeen of the stunned population and clean out the assay office, stealing $75,000 worth of freshly mined gold. A group of vigilantes led by Don Plunkett give chase, determined to dispense some Old West justice.

Eddie Carter is mistaken for a gang member and to escape a lynching he must go on the run, handcuffed to outlaw leader Dave Mooney, the man responsible for the death of his partner.

In the confrontation that follows, the stolen gold disappears with an outcome that nobody could have anticipated.

By the same author

Revenge at Powder River

A Gift from Crick

John McNally

ROBERT HALE

First published in Great Britain 2018

ISBN 978-0-7198-2812-6

The Crowood Press
The Stable Block
Crowood Lane
Ramsbury
Marlborough
Wiltshire SN8 2HR

www.bhwesterns.com

Robert Hale is an imprint
of The Crowood Press

Typeset by
Derek Doyle & Associates, Shaw Heath
Printed and bound in Great Britain by
4Bind Ltd, Stevenage, SG1 2XT

1

Let's start with Dave Mooney. Now Dave was mean, boy, was he mean. He was a man just spoiling for a fight. He had a temper sharper than a stropped razor. A man whose life was defined by the crimes he committed and the people he killed. He'd sure kicked up some dust in his time.

Then there was his brother Flem. Some folk said that Flem Mooney wasn't as bad as his brother Dave but that's like saying being mauled by a hungry bobcat is better than being bitten by an angry rattlesnake. He was still a nasty piece of work. He'd like as hit you just for stepping on his shadow.

And Fred Cooper, twenty-three years of spite and cruelty. He had a face off the far side of ugly. He looked like he'd been trapped, part skinned and left to die. He always wore a hat because he'd got some affliction that meant his hair just grew in clumps, like the coat of a dog with mange. Now there's an old saying that goes on about not judging a man until you've walked in his moccasins for two moons but you would not want to get inside Fred Cooper's mind. No, sir, not ever. You do not want to share the thoughts and feelings that stoked the furnace that always raged in his head.

Whatever you've done bad they've done it twice over, and then some.

You get the picture. Hell wouldn't know what hit it when they got there.

Now if old Walt Hollingsworth had not dropped dead that winter then his nephew Nate might still be alive today. But die Walt did and Nate took over his claim and brought his friend Eddie Carter along with him.

Early one morning the hidden man, Dave Mooney, stood like a dark secret in the deep pools of shadow under the trees. He looked down at the miner working by the water. A creek bed ran between two steep sided hills wet with springs and runoff that leaked out of the rocks. The miner knelt with his back to Mooney and poured water and dirt from the creek bed into an old rocker box. He rolled it backwards and forwards, sluicing the water through to separate any gold from the sand and gravel in the silt at the bottom of the box.

His rifle lay propped against a large rock maybe four paces behind him. His blue shirt was taut across his shoulders and dark with sweat, his hat pushed low on his head to shade his eyes as he crouched in concentration. The sun blazed overhead and heat waves rippled on the horizon; he paused to straighten and stretch his back. Way down the valley he saw a small weak dust devil swirl upwards, spin across the valley floor and break apart. He went back to work. It was August of 1852 and always hot at that time of year in Del Norte County, California.

Mooney brushed a fly out of his face with the back of his hand and waited. He glanced off to his right and studied the tent further down the slope, the canvas sun-bleached white over time, pitched by a clump of trees on a bright empty hillside where the ground sloped upwards into thick strands of pine.

A second miner sat by a fire pit in front of the tent and poured himself a coffee from a smoke-blackened tin pot. He sat back with his legs stretched out in front of him. Mooney saw his brother Flem and Fred Cooper edge out of the undergrowth behind the tent and close in on the coffee drinker.

The miners' horse and mule stood tethered in the shade by the tent. The horse was a shiny black Morgan, he looked up, swished his tail, shook his head and snorted. The miner by the fire roused himself and looked back over his shoulder at the horse. Fred Cooper ran forward and whacked him on the head with his gun butt and the man slumped forward like a sack of grain.

Dave Mooney watched the miner by the creek in front of him turn, stand up and look for his gun.

'Don't move, mister,' said Mooney in a deep voice that rolled down the hillside like thunder. He clicked the hammer back on his rifle and the miner jerked his head up and saw Mooney, a big man with a scarred face and a dark beard walk out of the sunlight across the shoulder of the hill towards him. He wore a blue chequered shirt and black corduroy trousers. Mooney lifted the rifle barrel as he moved and said,

'Don't go for that gun. Don't make me do what I'm thinking. Look at me, raise your hands or I'll put you down hard.'

Mooney could not see the miner's expression under the shade of his hat but the man raised his arms.

Fred Cooper shouted across, 'This one's out cold, Dave.'

Mooney nodded but kept his gaze locked on his prisoner, his eyes flat and cold, saying, 'Walk down the hill to the tent,' and they both moved off. As they got nearer he shouted across at Cooper, 'Why the hell did you slug him, Fred? We might need both of them to talk.' As he spoke, he prodded his prisoner in the back with his gun barrel then he drove the stock of the rifle into the man's kidney and knocked him to the ground.

Fred Cooper stooped and picked up a wooden pail half filled with water. He wore a black scuffed bowler hat jammed down on his head to cover his patchy hair and a sweat stained collarless grey shirt and baggy trousers. A small man with a mountain boy face, bleak and savage with pitiless eyes, Cooper scowled. His forehead creased in a rigid knot, he said, 'I guess I hit him because I didn't like the way he looked at me, Mooney.'

His eyes hollowed deep in his weathered face looked like two bullet holes in a burlap sack.

Dave's brother Flem spoke for the first time. 'Take it easy, Dave, he got the job done. They know we mean business now, don't they, Fred?'

'Damn right,' said Cooper. He swilled the unconscious miner with water, threw the bucket aside and pulled the groggy man to his feet by his hair.

Flem Mooney stepped up, grabbed a bunch of the man's shirt in his big calloused hand, shook him like a rag doll and forced him to his knees.

The two brothers Dave and Flem Mooney looked alike: tall, powerfully built, dark haired with the same large round face like a pie plate. Flem wore a big brush moustache. His brother Dave had a dark thick beard as smooth and black as an animal pelt, and a long sore looking scar running down the side of his face across his cheek and into his beard. It looked like someone had sliced his face off and stuck it back on again at an odd angle.

In fact, his brother Flem helped Dave get the scar. Well, they were half brothers really and that caused the problem in the first place. Dave was three when his pa remarried (no one ever told him what had happened to his ma). Flem came along soon afterwards and the boys grew up fighting, each other to start with but then back to back against anyone and everyone. Their pa told folk he did his goddamn best, he beat them good every single day of their lives when they were kids but they still turned out bad. Their ma said Pa got it all wrong, he should have fetched a belt to them as well as laying into them with his fists.

One fall, when they were young men they went out hunting bear up by the headwaters of the Rogue River, down the south side of Crater Lake if you know the area. Dave shot a black bear. Young Flem tried to look pleased but felt jealous as hell. Now that black bear was a mean old boy, he went down hard in a cloud of dust and stink but as Dave moved in, he lashed out a huge paw, dragged Dave down and started to maul him, trying hard to crush his skull. Flem raised his gun but thought better of it, brother Dave bragged he was tough so he decided to let him handle the bear. Luckily for Dave a couple of passing hunters heard the ruckus, waded in and killed the bear. Dave survived, of course, with a scar to prove it. Flem always claimed his gun jammed up but there were days when Dave looked at Flem with murder in his eyes.

Not yet today though, it was still early, but for now he had work to do and money to make.

A saddle creaked and two riders walked their horses out of the trees, they both rode with rifles propped on their thighs. Dave Mooney pushed his gun barrel deep into his prisoner's back and said, 'Don't get your hopes up, mister; them boys are with us.'

Flem Mooney looked irritated, he stared at his brother Dave, deep wrinkles meshed his face, and he pressed his lips together in a tight line and said, 'Come on, Dave, let's get to it and get gone. We've been in these parts too long, it's getting too hot for us. We've been grubbing around, taking bits and pieces of gold off the likes of these two and got no more than a few dollars to show for it. Let's make them squeal and move on, I hear there's plenty of gold not far from here at a place called Sailors Diggings up in Oregon territory.'

'Right,' said Cooper, nodding. He looked at Dave Mooney and added, 'Maybe we've been following you too long.'

Dave Mooney looked hard at Cooper and took a step towards him.

'Seems like you want to take charge, Fred, is that it?'

A brittle tension grew in the silence around them. Cooper stared at Mooney, his gaze locked on his face like he was looking down the barrel of a carbine.

'Maybe it's time I did run things,' Cooper said.

'For Christ's sake, will you two stop kicking?' said Flem. He wore a red plaid shirt with dark sweat stains under the arms, he rolled his shirt sleeves up to his elbows, drew his Colt Walker and pointed it at the miner kneeling in the dirt, whose hair and skin was freckled with grit. To the miner he said, 'Where's your gold? Tell us right quick and we might let you be.'

Flem cocked his gun with his thumb, the noise like a dry twig snapping. He scowled and his dark face smouldered with impatience, he jammed his gun barrel under the miner's jaw and pushed his head back with it. 'What are you going to do, mister, give it up or roll the dice? It's your call.'

The miner stared at the gun barrel with the look of a man hanging off a cliff edge by his fingertips, and he spoke in a dry voice as if his mouth was full of dirt. 'We ain't got much, it's bagged up and covered by a big rock under the fire. Take it and go.'

Flem Mooney smiled and said, 'See, that wasn't too hard now, was it?'

They watched Cooper sweep the fire aside with his boot, lift a rock, pull a small sack out and heft it in his left hand. His eyes glittered with pleasure, he drew his own gun and shot the kneeling miner in the guts. The pain raced through the miner's body and exploded in excruciating agony; he sat down heavily in the dust, one hand pressed against the wound in his stomach. He looked down and watched bright red blood ooze between his fingers.

Fred Cooper laughed. 'See, Dave, it was worth me putting a knot in his head, we got it done double quick.' His voice hardened. 'And listen good, I decide who I hit and who I kill, not you.'

The gun shot raised a squall of birds out of the trees and echoed across the hillside. They heard someone shout up in the woods and another call off to their left across the river.

'Come on,' said Cooper, 'time to skedaddle right sharp before their neighbours come down to see what all the palaver is.'

They heard a boot scrape on gravel and turned to see the other miner make a run for the river. The two men sitting on their horses opened fire. The first rider's shot ricocheted off a rock close to the running man, he stumbled but kept going. A second shot went high and wide as the miner zigzagged closer to the water's edge, it looked as though he might make it. Dave Mooney swung his rifle up, pushed the stock into his shoulder and fired. The miner cried out and fell as the shot took him low in the back. He pitched forward and lay face down on the rocks.

The two riders cantered down with the other horses and the Mooney brothers and Cooper mounted up in silence, rode up the slope and disappeared into the darkness of the woods, leaving a deathly hush on the hillside.

Dave Mooney rode behind Fred Cooper, he always did. He'd heard stories about Cooper many times and figured the best place to keep a mad dog was in front of you. Only last week they'd run from Silver City because Cooper argued with two men in Johnny Ward's Dance Hall. Cooper stabbed one of the men, chased the other out into the street and shot him in the neck then, sullen faced, he walked back in and ordered another drink. Mooney didn't mind killing folk but he just didn't trust Cooper, he was as moody as a scorpion with a belly ache. Cooper's wildness meant they had to move three ways from Sunday most times and high-tail it before they could make any real money. Mooney felt pretty sure he'd have to kill Cooper one day soon and that thought made him feel a whole lot better.

2

The miner by the water was still alive. He was Eddie Carter. He lay and drifted in and out of consciousness. He heard the gunmen ride off but he could not move, his back felt as if a mule had kicked him. He knew his friend Nate lay gut shot behind him and needed his help but a great tiredness seeped through his body and its heaviness pressed down on him and drained him of energy.

He smelled the coldness of the water by his face, closed his eyes and his mind drifted back four years to the first time he met Nate Hollingsworth and how Hollingsworth saved his life.

Back then, Carter scouted for the Army, chasing down Cayuse Indians in a mind-numbing campaign that dragged on for six months or more. They camped by a box canyon off the Hood River, forty miles or so out of the log fort at Camp Drum.

A company sergeant, he couldn't remember his name, told him to scout the northern ridge with another civilian scout, Nate Hollingsworth. He explained where to find Hollingsworth and told them to slip out at dusk and get the lie of the land for the morning charge.

Carter pushed through some black gooseberry bushes and found Hollingsworth sat by a fire under a wild plum tree near the banks of the river, cooking fatback on a skillet. He looked about forty, wore a slouch hat pinned up at the front, a gloomy bag of a man with a sad leathery face and dark, deep watchful eyes. They liked each other right off and shared the food, cornbread and fried ham, and a coffee made of chicory and acorn that wasn't half bad. They grumbled about the Army like regulars and talked into the late afternoon. Carter did not say much about himself, generally he kept tight lipped on where he had been and what he had done, he reckoned that was his business.

They set off as the sky dimmed but it took a long time for the night to arrive, the dark seemed to come in really slowly as if it struggled against the wind. They rode out of the trees and through rocky dry ravines spiked with brush. Eventually they left their horses and climbed a steep canyon side on foot, the high ridge silhouetted in the fading light like jagged tin.

At the top they bellied down and peeped over the rim where the valley floor sloped down from the canyon entrance to a rock wall streaked with shadow. They saw two large fires and heard the steady thump of the Cayuse drums beating out an eerie lament. The sweat poured off Hollingsworth, his upper lip beaded in moisture; he kept wiping his mouth and nose with the palm of his hand.

'We've seen enough, let's get back, something ain't right,' he whispered. He started back to the horses without waiting for Carter. He almost ran across the clearing and pulled his horse reins off a tangled bush.

Carter paused to look around and saw the shadow of a man detach itself from the rocks above Hollingsworth and drop like a stone. A knife blade glinted in the moonlight. Carter drew his Colt and fired in one smooth movement and the Cayuse brave crumpled without a sound. Three more shadows dashed out from the boulders as the two scouts leaped onto their horses and kicked them into action, the horse hoofs tore at the ground and threw out great clods of earth. All they could hear was the heavy laboured breathing of the horses as they whipped them up the incline to safety.

Carter felt something solid and hard hit him as an arrow thumped into him and caught him high in the shoulder. A searing pain scorched down his arm and he grunted, swayed and almost fell from his saddle. He struggled to find his balance and his horse slowed but then he felt Hollingsworth grab his wrist, straighten him in the saddle, sweep up his reins and drag him and his horse clear. They kicked for camp, let their horses have a loose rein and rode hard enough to outrun their own shadows.

He collapsed when they got back to camp but remembered how Hollingsworth had overcome his own fear to help him, hell, he'd saved his life. . . .

'Eddie, can you hear me? Wake up.'

Carter opened his eyes in confusion.

'Nate, is that you?' he said in a puzzled murmur, his hazy mind still caught in his memories from their past.

'Nate's dead,' said the voice. 'Took one in the belly and bled out by the time I got here. Looks like you're going be fine and dandy though.' Carter squinted against the light and saw Arnie Short, a neighbouring placer with a claim further along, bending over him. Short was little more than a kid, small, and thin enough to be made of wire with dirty blond hair, a snub nose and jug ears.

'I plugged your wound and tied it tight, Eddie. The bullet went clean through your side, made maybe a two inch tunnel.' He paused and wiped his hands down the sides of his trousers. 'I buried Nate over by the trees with a view of the mountains. Sorry, I didn't have no words to say over him. He was a fine man and deserved better.'

Carter struggled to sit up, he felt the bandages tight around his waist.

'Them's fine words, Arnie, they'll do,' he said.

Carter looked about to say more when they both heard a wagon and team draw off the track and push through the trees. It looked hard going for the wagon but the driver brought them in. He sat in the shade for a moment and then flicked his reins across the backs of the mules, clicked his tongue and came out into the light. Birds squawked and flapped deep in the shadows, the grass grew tall and green up by the tree line and Carter watched two big boned mules and a canvas topped wagon sway out across the rough ground. The wagon looked fully loaded, the iron rims on the hickory wood-spoked wheels cut the ground and gouged tracks through the coarse grass out from the shade of the trees.

The driver was Quincy Roof, a decent family man. His fourteen-year-old daughter Bethenia married a slacker called Legrand Hill and they had a baby named Henry. Quincy bought them a farm but Hill gambled and lost the farm to foreclosure. Then Quincy and his wife gave them some land and built a cabin on it for them. Quincy had a store in Marysville, Polk County. Now to help support his daughter and pay for the land, he needed to raise extra cash so he spent his summers in his wagon selling goods to the settlements and camps along the west coast while his wife stayed and minded the store.

'Hello, the camp,' said Roof. He stopped and waited. 'I heard shooting and thought I'd best come by and see if anyone needed help.'

Roof was a small man with a long grey beard that ran down onto his chest, and he wore a lumpy brown suit with a short brimmed hat. He raised the hat in greeting and he was as bald as a skinned onion. He held the reins one handed and gripped a scattergun in his right. When he saw the two men by the tent he relaxed, stretched back and put the gun in the wagon. He looked Carter over and said, 'Can I come in, friends? The name's Quincy Roof. I sell the best quality goods on the west coast. You sure look like you could do with a coffee and some grub.'

Carter shrugged and said, 'Come on in. I'm Eddie Carter and this young feller is Arnie Short.' His dry throat made his voice gravelly. He took a deep breath and the heat went out of his face.

Roof nodded to Short and studied Carter. He saw that he was hurt and suffering; his tired eyes did not look at anyone, he just stared off into the distance. Carter was maybe twenty-five or so, average height, clean shaved, friendly looking with bright blue eyes webbed with tiny lines at the corners. Roof watched him on the opposite side of the fire, favouring his left side with his hand pressed against his hip.

'You hurt?'

'Seems that way. That'll be the shots you heard. Five men. Killed my partner and rode out that way.' He pointed to a rutted track that wound through the woods with a thick canopy of branches and a layer of pine needles and dead leaves on the ground.

Quincy Roof ran a hand down his beard and waited, he saw the grass by the fire flattened and stippled with blood dried on the dirt in reddish patches. The wagon axles ticked in the shade, he climbed down and the wagon boards creaked as his weight shifted. He caught sight of the newly dug ground and the grave mound.

'You boys sit right there, I'm going to see to my mules and then I'll cook us up some food.'

Carter laid back on a tangle of grass and put an arm across his eyes. His back throbbed and the pain seemed to leech away his energy and he drifted off to sleep.

The smell of fresh coffee and meat cooking woke him up. He propped himself on his elbows and Roof poured a coffee, laced it with molasses and passed it across, squinting through the smoke. He laid a pan across the flames and broke eight eggs into it and served them with grits. Roof grunted.

'I heard the shots and riders heading out, riding hard enough to wear the hoofs off their horses.' He took off his old derby hat and fanned the flames with it.

'Figure I'll find them and settle things,' said Carter.

'You look like you've been trampled by horses. What are you aiming to do, ride in and faint all over them?' Roof said and smiled.

'I'll go now and I'll rest up tonight, they're heading for Sailors Diggings. Them killers don't give two nothings about what happens to anybody else but they'll be dead this time tomorrow if I get my way.'

They ate in silence then Roof looked up, straightened his jacket and said, 'I'll patch you up proper if you like. I've bandages and a liniment that can seal the holes in an old boot. Cartridges too if you've got the money. I see you've got a Colt Navy and a Sharps carbine in your saddle boot. Well, I've got foil cartridges for the Colt with twenty-five grains of powder in them and paper ones for the carbine.'

Carter said, 'I've used paper before. How does that foil work?'

'Well,' said Roof, 'I ain't no expert but the powder and bullet are wrapped in the foil and it's waterproof. The flame from the cap goes through the foil, sets the powder off and spits the bullet out. Easy, fast to load and guaranteed to fire. If it don't fire you get your money back.'

'If you're still alive.'

'Well, there is that.' Both men laughed but Arnie Short's washed out eyes clouded over with worry, his young face pink with heat.

'Listen, Eddie,' Arnie said, 'I don't like it. Meanness don't happen overnight, that's how they are and always have been is my guess. Hard men are used to gun play. There's five of them and one of you. It's like running against a pack of wolves.'

'The boy's right,' said Roof, 'doing what's right don't mean nothing to them. They've killed your friend and shot you in the back.'

'It'll work out different next time. I've been pushed around before and they lived to regret it. I cain't rest until I make it right for Nate, I've got to do it.'

Carter ate his meal and bought some beef jerky, a wide belt and cartridges for his two handguns and his rifle, a Sharps Saddle Ring. He pulled the belt as tight as he could around his waist to hold his bandages in place and support the wound. He said no to the liniment. He decided to rest for ten minutes before he set off and stretched out with his head on his saddle. He lit a cigar and watched the smoke curled upwards and break apart in the breeze.

Roof played with his beard and never stopped talking, he began some tale about the cost of beef at the Angel Camp in Calaveras County compared to Sam Brannan's store in Sacramento when Carter's head started to dip. His eyes closed and his head kept nodding forward before he jerked it back. He sat up a little and tried opening his eyes wide but he drifted until he could not stop himself closing his eyes and gliding into sleep.

When he woke he saw from the sun's position it was well into the afternoon.

'We let you sleep,' said Roof. He held up a hand. 'No, don't say it. You looked as comfy as a goat in a nettle patch. You needed to rest, you know you did.' He stretched across and handed Carter a tin plate heaped high with fried beans and spicy sausage.

'You're right,' said Carter, his voice sounded thick and tired but he started to eat. He knew that he needed to get after them but saw no point going all out at it. He realized that he needed to build up his strength.

He felt guilty that he had not been able to save Nate's life and then he decided to stop apologizing over and over again to him in his own mind. He remembered an old Army trooper he scouted with who used to say when someone died, 'Look, he's dead, we're sorry. Now get back out there and kill someone for him.' Carter realized that he wanted to kill Nate's murderers because he felt ashamed that he hadn't been able to save him.

Carter turned when he realized that Roof was speaking.

'I'm heading to Sailors Diggings myself. I'm a regular there, they know me well. Ride with me a piece, why don't you?'

'No, thanks, I need to make up some time. I don't want to lose their trail.'

'Suit yourself, you don't want to lose your life though.'

Roof watched Carter, he seemed a decent sort but he had a look about him that made Roof uneasy but he couldn't say why. Finally it occurred to him that Carter was willing to die as long as he could take some of the killers with him along the way.

'Why not let them go, partner? You're wounded and there's five of them, there must be a better way than this. Why not take the easy life?'

'I don't want an easy life, I just want to be quick enough with a gun to survive the one I've got.' His eyes looked as bitter as strong black coffee. 'Is there a lawman in Sailors Diggings?'

Roof shook his head and said, 'No, I reckon justice is paid out in gunfire and bullets.'

Carter shrugged his shoulders.

'The more I see the more I reckon that shooting is the only law we have in these parts. We might not like it but it's all we've got. That's all there is to it.'

Arnie Short said, 'What are you going to do now, Eddie? You cain't take on the five of them.' He watched Carter run his hand down his chin and stare off into the distance, lost in thought. The lines around his eyes and across his forehead deepened and looked like dry and rugged tracks. Finally he nodded to himself.

'Listen, Arnie, I know your claim ain't up to much.' Short started to speak but Carter continued. 'No, hear me out. Don't worry none. You can be my new partner on this here claim, you deserve it for your help today. You work it while I'm gone. I've a score to settle for Nate first,' He pointed with his chin over to the fresh grave. He struggled to his feet and tightened the gun rig on his hip. He took out the Colt and looked down at it. It had a brass back strap and trigger guard, he ran a hand over the barrel frame and hammer and they looked plum blue in the shadow of his body. He spun the cylinder, looking for the glint of the firing caps in each chamber as they ticked by one at a time before he holstered the gun.

He picked up a black hat with a round hard brim and a low crown. He punched and shaped the crown, fitted it on his head and settled his gun belt on his hips.

'If I don't come back this claim's yours, give me a week or so. We might not have a lot to say over Nate but I'll find the men who did this and nail their hides to the nearest barn door. I'll try my damnedest and just have to hope my damnedest is good enough. We'll let my gun do the talking, it's the only language some folk understand. I'll just go in hard, shoot straight and pull them all down. Believe it.'

As the outlaw Dave Mooney crossed from California into Oregon he paused, it felt like a cold hand just gripped his heart for a moment. He looked back but the trail was clear. He shrugged, kicked on and followed the other gang members towards Sailors Diggings.

Fifty miles or so back down the trail, Eddie Carter picked up their tracks and set off to chase them down.

3

The five-man Mooney gang rode into Sailors Diggings, a mining settlement near the head waters of the Illinois River just south of Cave Junction in Oregon territory, a few miles north of the California state line.

Aside from Dave and Flem Mooney and Fred Cooper, there were two other men with them, Chris Stover and Miles Horn. They were handy with a gun and the right amount of red liquor made them a couple of tough critters. But they were more thieves than outright murderers like the others. You still wouldn't want to bump into them down some alleyway on a dark night though.

Chris Stover was a crook for sure, he served as a deputy sheriff in Yamhill County but they ran him out of town because they thought he was a horse thief; they were right on that score.

Miles Horn worked a variety of jobs, he ended up

breaking a leg in a coal slip. When the leg mended he was near starving and took to thieving. He had the gormless look of a stupid mule, they said his mind moved slower than Mississippi mud.

The five of them found the livery, left their horses and headed for the nearest saloon. A wide boardwalk ran down the dusty street, the planking creaked with the heat and the thick smell of hot dust and horse sweat clotted the air. They went into the Rusty Nail saloon because it was open twenty-four hours a day. A long dull panelled bar, made of oak, ran the width of the room across the cigarette burned timber floor sticky with tobacco spit.

They trailed across the room in a line that oozed hostility. Several regular drinkers glanced their way but quickly found something more interesting to look at in the bottom of their glass.

They sat at a corner table and Flem Mooney brought over a bottle of Forty Rod whiskey. He took his jacket off, hung it on the back of the chair and loosened the top button on his red plaid shirt and they set to drinking it. Cooper threw the first glass back and sighed.

'That's good deadshot. Drinking a lot of Forty Rod's like getting punched, it burns when it hits you, fogs your mind and then you're out like a light. Perfect.'

Dave Mooney took his tobacco pouch out of his jacket pocket and casually tossed it on the table. He concentrated on rolling his cigarette and only looked up as he ran his tongue along the paper. He struck a match on the rough board table and lit up. The cigarette paper flared in flame and he blew it, watched until it died to a glowing ember then he took a pull and held it in his mouth while he watched the others through the smoke. He let them settle before he spoke.

'I'll go down to the assay office and sell the gold we've got. There's around two pounds that should fetch maybe $600.' The cigarette bobbed in his mouth as he spoke.

'Jesus H Christ, Dave, that ain't much for a week of killing,' said Flem Mooney.

'Less than $100 a killing I reckon,' said Fred Cooper. 'That ain't hardly worth the lead.'

Flem looked at his brother and scratched at a spot on his throat, the others waited for him to speak.

'Listen, Dave,' said Flem, 'me and the boys talked some, we all agree it's time I ran things.' He smiled as he spoke but his eyes were icy and intense, he looked taut enough to snap. He laid his hands on the table, they were big and square like sawn lumber and as rough as tree bark. 'I think we need to hold up a bank or something. Make a whole lot of money.'

Cooper nodded, leaned back, hooked his thumbs in his gun belt, looked Dave Mooney in the eye and said, 'Any objections, us getting shed of you?'

Dave Mooney sighed and tried to look bored. He glanced at Chris Stover. Stover had a narrow pock-marked face, arms and legs as thin as a rail and he was so tall his legs looked too long for his body.

'Chris?'

'I'm with Flem, like he said we all agreed it,' said Stover, looking hard at the animal antlers racked above the bar rather than meet his eyes.

He glanced over at Miles Horn, a morose man who looked to be made up of spare parts with a large nose, small chin and bad teeth that he tried to hide with a big drooping moustache. He had a face that only a mother could love. Horn hardly ever spoke. He just shrugged his thin shoulders and looked away.

'Don't make it hard, Dave,' said Flem Mooney, 'and I'd feel better if you put your hands where we can see them, you hear?'

'No,' Dave Mooney said, throwing the word down real hard as a challenge but Flem did not dare to pick it up. Dave did not move, he enjoyed letting the tension build, he thought about slamming his hand on the table for the hell of it and watch them all fall about but he decided they weren't worth the effort. The scar on his cheek shone a livid red, he brought his right hand out, without hurrying, scratched his beard and ran a finger down the scar tissue. He blinked slowly.

'If that's the way you want it I'll leave,' he said. 'I'll cash the gold and let you get about your business.' He pushed his chair away with the back of his legs and stood up.

Fred Cooper drew a gun and held it flat on the table with his hand on the butt and his finger across the trigger. Mooney glanced at the gun, leaned forward with his hands propped on the table, his knuckles round and hard. He said, 'Put that back in your rig, Cooper or I'll shove it down your throat sideways.'

Cooper flushed and his eyes glowed like a mad dog.

'Put it away, Fred,' said Stover, putting an arm around Cooper's shoulders. 'We're all friends here ... more or less.'

Dave Mooney snorted and gave a deep nasty laugh that went on too long. He turned, went out and left them to their drinking.

Outside Mooney walked to the edge of the settlement and just before the livery, found the assay office, a two storey clapper board building with large glass windows on either side of the door. Inside he crossed to the counter where an old timer in faded overalls and a strap undershirt stood and waited to be paid out. The clerk fiddled with the scales and mumbled in a bored voice.

'That's $300.' He opened a drawer under the counter and laid the money out. The old timer picked it up and went out without speaking. The clerk dropped the gold into box behind him and said to a second clerk, 'There he goes, George, the same every week, straight to the Lucky Legend. He'll have nothing left by tomorrow morning.'

'Pity he doesn't save enough for a bath,' said George, holding his nose.

Mooney looked the place over, behind the polished timber counter stood an old desk and a chair pushed up tight against the back wall. Next to it was a closed door that led to a back room. The second clerk, George, sat at the desk and looked to be working in a big bound ledger, the shelf above the desk thick with papers and boxes. The clerk on the counter turned and looked up at Mooney, his eyes lingered on Mooney's scarred face.

'Bear,' said Mooney.

'Pardon?' said the clerk, a young man with hollow cheeks and skin as white and smooth as a petticoat.

'My face,' said Mooney, making a claw of his hand. 'A bear.' The clerk's eyes dropped with embarrassment and two pools of red lit his pale cheeks. The second clerk glanced around then turned back and ducked his head towards the ledger.

Mooney put three bags of gold on the counter, the clerk weighed them and said, 'Twenty-two ounces, that's $440.'

He kept his eyes on the scales, fumbled under the counter and pushed the notes across without looking up. Mooney counted them, taking his time, folded the money into his jacket pocket while his hunter's eyes missed nothing and gave nothing away.

'I'll see you again,' he said, staring with the empty eyes of a hungry red-tailed hawk. He turned and left, closing the door with care.

He stood on the sidewalk. The plan that occurred to him inside the assay office became clearer in his mind and the excitement burned through him and lit up his face. He knew how to bring real money in and with luck, teach the rest of his gang a lesson they would never forget. He would get them to rob the assay office and then he would steal the gold from them.

He called at the store and spent some time at the livery and maybe an hour or so later, he walked back to the saloon, trying hard not to smirk.

4

Inside the Rusty Nail saloon they worked hard at their drinking. When Dave Mooney sat he saw that all four of them burned with a whiskey flush, their faces bright with sweat and their voices dull with drink. As Miles Horn talked, he struck a match, held it to his cigarette and the flame lit up the red and blue veins that threaded his cheeks.

'Come on, Dave, have a drink with us.' His voice sounded full of rust and deep wrinkles meshed his face. He pushed a chair across with his foot and Mooney sat, picked up the nearest glass and drained it.

'Hand over my money,' said Fred Cooper in a harsh voice, staring at Dave Mooney. His face looked overheated as he boiled in his own juices.

Mooney struck like an angry snake; he whipped his gun out and the Colt barrel sliced the air. With a vicious thud it hit Cooper's head and he went down like a bag of nails. Miles Horn reached across for Cooper's glass and finished his drink.

'He's going to be real sore at you when he wakes up,' said Flem Mooney in a couldn't care less voice.

'What's new?' said Dave Mooney. 'Here's your money, forty dollars apiece. Reckon I'll be off.'

'Whoa, Dave,' said Chris Stover. 'Like Miles said, stay and have a drink.'

Mooney stayed and drank with them, going glass for glass, waiting for Cooper to come around before he told them his plan. Flem Mooney picked Cooper up, threw him in a chair and laid his head on the plank table. What a poor excuse for men, Dave Mooney thought, as he looked at them over the rim of his glass. They all carried on drinking, the air dense with the smell of sweaty clothes and bodies laced with tobacco smoke.

Cooper was less trouble than they expected when he woke up. He sat up and rolled his neck, coughed a hacking sound deep in his chest and just carried on drinking. His eyes held an aggressive glint like an angry bear, but he did not speak. What with the drink and the wallop on the head, Cooper's face looked a picture of confusion. There were three other drinks lined up in front of him.

'They're yours, Fred and here's forty dollars,' said Flem Mooney.

'I've got even better news for all of you,' Dave Mooney said. 'Listen good.' He dropped his voice and almost laughed out loud when the four men leaned forward like hogs at a trough. He held a cigarette between two fingers and he pointed with it at the men around the table. 'I've got one last job for all of us if you're interested and then I'll quit for good.'

'We're listening,' said Chris Stover in a thick voice, his long face and narrow shoulders hunched over his glass.

'This settlement's alive with placers, they're all over the hills, there's a goddamn gold rush on. I've been inside the assay office down by the livery. My guess is that the back room is full of gold. As far as I can see there's only two men working in there and they're just a pair of scrub faced Bible pushers.'

'What have you got in mind?' said Stover; he glanced at Flem Mooney but turned back to his brother Dave and waited.

'Well, I'll keep it simple for you, boys,' said Dave Mooney. 'We bust in, grab what we can and get a whole lot of gone between us and this place. Can you follow that?'

'Hey, nobody don't talk to me like that,' said his brother Flem. 'We get it and I'll run it.'

Flem Mooney held a cigarette between yellowed fingers and squinted through layers of drifting smoke. His face glowed with drink and his unshaved jaw looked to be filmed with black grit. Dave Mooney looked across and saw the jealous little boy he'd fought with for twenty years.

'Whatever you want, brother,' said Dave Mooney. 'Listen, I already bought some old grain sacks from the store to carry the gold and I've hired a mule to carry it, it's down at the livery. Hell, don't you worry none about me, I'll follow you ... this last time.'

Fred Cooper spoke up, he slurred his first few words, paused and tried again.

'Right, let's get to it. But Flem runs it. Dave, you do as you're told. I ain't forgot that you put a knot in my head and when this is over, you need to get gone or you'll have me to answer to.'

'That sounds like a promise you know you can't keep,' said Dave Mooney, his eyes scorched with anger and alcohol.

Cooper sat and clenched his fists; they could hear the rage build inside his shallow breathing. They saw his sunken cheeks, tiny pointed teeth and dark baleful eyes but none of them could hear the whirring in his head like a hornets nest. Flem Mooney laid a hand on Cooper's arm and said, 'Leave it, Fred, we got a whole lot on our minds right now. Get the gold then you sort out your differences, you hear me on that? Let's stick together, we need all the guns we can get. We finish the bottle and check we're all loaded.' He looked at his brother. 'Will you stop riling, Dave, you're getting on my wrong side right quick.'

'The sooner we get it done the sooner we go our own ways,' said Dave Mooney. He took off his hat and ran his hand through his thick dark hair. And the sooner you boys ride to hell, he thought, putting his hat back on, slanted on his forehead and low over his eyes.

5

'Right,' said Flem Mooney, 'here's how it plays out.' He ran a finger around the inside of his empty glass and licked it. 'We all go down to this assay office. Miles, you cover the door from the inside while the rest of us get the gold. You see anything that don't smell right, you holler—'

Dave Mooney interrupted, 'There's windows each side of the door onto the street.'

Flem stared at him with his lips pressed together and his eyes riveted on him as he spoke. 'So if anyone comes you'll see them. Miles, you let them come on in then shove your gun in their face and get them sat on the floor.'

Horn nodded.

'We fill the bags, lock the two men from the office in the back room and we get gone down the road without anyone knowing we've been there.'

'Wait,' said Stover, 'are we bringing the horses up from the livery?'

'No,' said Flem Mooney. His face and moustache flared in the cupped flame of a match as he lit another cigarette. 'See, we don't want anyone figuring there's anything going on, we need to be in and out without making a fuss.'

Dave Mooney tapped the table with his glass and said, 'How about I go next door to the livery? I can saddle up once we've got the gold and bring the horses up to the back.'

Stover nodded. 'That makes sense, we wait in the office once we're done and give Dave a couple of minutes to sort out the horses and then we walk out back.'

'Meantimes, we deal with anyone who turns up,' said Flem Mooney, wiping the drink off his moustache with his wrist.

'Kill them you mean,' said Cooper with a grin.

'No, Fred,' said Flem in a quiet voice, 'we don't want no commotion. We hold them and crack a few heads before we leave. You with me on that, Fred?'

'I hear you,' said Cooper, draining his glass and wiping his mouth with his sleeve. He had three hand guns, two in his rig and a big Colt Walker he took out of his waistband and shoved into the front of his shirt across his stomach. He lurched to his feet and steadied himself with his hands on the table. 'Let's go pick some cotton,' he said.

Miles Horn bit a lump out of a plug of tobacco, wadded it into his cheek and with his jaw packed tight began to chew. He smiled, showing a mouthful of bad teeth brown with tobacco juice.

They all started to move.

'Cooper,' said Dave Mooney in a low voice, 'take that daft look off your face, don't do nothing mule headed. Like Flem said, you keep it simple and quiet.'

Cooper's slit eyes burned with resentment but before he could speak, the others headed for the door. Cooper stood as tight as a coiled spring aching for release. He drained his glass and felt the alcohol spread through his brain like someone whispering in his ear and the rage built like a hot oven in his head until his mind fairly hummed with fury. He cussed under his breath and half ran after the others, his hand on his Colt Walker. His eyes, level and unblinking, stared straight at Dave Mooney's broad back.

Mooney walked a couple of paces in front of him, the others already on the street. Mooney's big body stood silhouetted in the doorway and Cooper felt the anger well up and overflow, flooding his brain. He drew the gun out of his shirt and thumbed back the hammer. As Mooney left, he let the doors swing back and they hit Cooper, who stumbled, lurched upright and burst out of the door like a rabid dog.

He lifted the gun as he came outside, the sun reflected off the windows opposite like pools of fire. He blinked with the glare and pulled the trigger.

Dave Mooney had stepped down off the boardwalk into the powdery street. Three strangers turned into the saloon doorway as Fred Cooper rushed out and fired. Cooper's shot took the first man square in the chest and the blow from the big Colt bullet slammed him backwards and he fell without a sound. The smoke from the shot filled the air and the shade under the veranda hung heavy with the smell of it. There was a moment of stunned silence and then the dead man's friends backed away a pace, shouted in confused outrage and drew their guns.

Cooper saw them draw and the Colt bucked in his hand, he struggled to bring it back in line and fired twice more. In the confined space the sound thundered against the walls and the air exploded with smoke and flame. The two men went down hard, one with a stomach wound and the other with a bullet in the groin. He thrashed his legs on the floor for a moment and died.

All hell broke loose in the street. Men shouted, women screamed and everyone ran for cover. Cooper stood in a cloud of gun smoke and cordite, a huge grin lit up his face like a Jack-o'-Lantern. Dave Mooney ran down the street, not sure what had happened but when shooting starts behind you, he reckoned, you high-tailed out of there and thought about it later.

A few of the men on the street fired at Cooper, peppering the front of the saloon. A post by Cooper's head splintered from a shot, the old wood gouged white by the bullet. Cooper felt a sharp pain on his face as the splinter nicked him and flicked a thread of blood across his forehead. He ducked and ran into the street.

Flem Mooney, Miles Horn and Chris Stover turned and saw Cooper racing down the street towards them, taking fire from all sides. They all drew their guns without hesitation and opened up on the bystanders, blasting anyone they could see. At least four men and one woman were caught in the hail of lead and lay dead or moaned with pain.

Dave Mooney fired into a crowd and his deep voice boomed above the noise.

'Get the hell away, all of you,' he shouted and the five gunmen ran for the livery.

Gunfire chased them down the street as more men poured out of the saloon and store and took up the fight. As they passed the assay office, Dave Mooney shouted, 'Inside, let's finish what we started.'

He kicked the door open and they all crowded in. A miner at the counter half turned and Fred Cooper shot him in the face.

Dave Mooney stepped over the body and grabbed the counter clerk, knotted his shirt in his big calloused fist, and slammed his head down hard against the wood. Chris Stover slid across the counter on his backside, drew his gun and shoved it in the second clerk's frightened face.

'Where's the gold?' he screamed.

The clerk swallowed, his eyes wide with fear.

'In the strong room at the back,' he said, his voice shaking as a nerve pulsed in his throat.

'Open it,' said Stover in a quiet cold voice.

'The key's on the table over there,' the clerk said and pointed with his head.

Flem Mooney vaulted the counter, took the key, opened the door and stepped inside. They heard him whistle in surprise.

'Looks like we're going to need big bags, boys,' he called over his shoulder.

Dave Mooney dragged the clerk over the counter, threw him on the floor and gave him a savage kick in the ribs.

'Watch him,' he said to Horn and he lifted the counter flap and went to the strong room. He pulled a couple of burlap sacks from his coat pocket as he went in.

'Looks like we struck a real gold vein, brother,' said Flem and they started to fill the sacks with the nuggets and dust lining the shelves.

They all heard the shouts from the street but there was no gunfire. Dave Mooney tied the full sacks with twine and hauled them into the front office.

'There's a passel of folk coming down this way,' said Cooper, looking out of the window, his blood-shot eyes flashing with excitement. He started to reload one of his guns.

Dave Mooney hefted the two sacks, one in each hand onto his big shoulders.

'Christ,' he said, 'there must be over a hundred pounds of gold here.' He puffed his cheeks and blew out his breath. With his thick neck corded with veins, his shoulders wide and sloping, his eyebrows a dark uninterrupted line and his dark beard, he looked like a monstrous shadow.

'I'll give you a hand,' said Stover.

'No,' Mooney said, a little too quickly in a voice as brittle and sharp as flint. He quietened his tone. 'I'll need all of you to cover me while I sort out the horses and the mule.'

Flem Mooney studied him for a moment, he bit down on his lower lip then nodded and moved to stand next to Chris Stover and Fred Cooper.

'Give them hell, boys,' he said. 'I'll hold back and shoot when you two need to reload. Miles, we got no cause to be quiet. Now shoot the two you're holding back there.'

The two clerks looked ashen. Horn hesitated then pointed with his gun barrel to the back room and the men ducked inside. He slammed and locked the door then strode to the front. He stepped onto the sidewalk, drew his second gun and opened up with both of them onto the crowd outside.

'You're heck on wheels, Miles, right enough,' said Cooper, who moved next to him and started shooting. 'Let's have us a hog killing time.'

Dave Mooney went past them, struggling with the weight of gold in the sacks. He disappeared down the alley to the back of the livery stables.

The shots from the assay office ripped into the crowd in the street, the air layered with dust, gun smoke and death. Blood stained the street and the smell of it rose in a clammy shroud. A woman cried and a man screamed in agony.

The remaining townsfolk turned and ran, they pushed, shoved and trampled anyone who got in their way. Horn and Cooper backed into the building to reload. Behind them Flem Mooney threw a chair through a front window and showered the sidewalk with glass. He stood silhouetted in the opening and waited. He saw a head rise up behind a water trough, and he fired and the head ducked back out of sight.

A shot from the street shattered the other window and blew the glass across the office floor. Flem Mooney crunched across to the empty window frame and shot a man kneeling by a barrel across the street.

The noise of the gunfire rolled out from the settlement and climbed the valley sides. Miners from the surrounding hills started to stream down from their workings into the settlement. They ran from the rocks and trees or rode down on mules and horses, they held hand guns or rifles across their chests as they came. Grim faced, they hollered and called to each other and gathered together in front of the saloon to hear what had happened.

'Chris,' said Flem Mooney, concentrating on the street, 'get on down the side of the building and cover the back, you hear?'

Stover went out of the door and ran in a crouch down between the buildings.

A few minutes later he rushed back, leaned in through the broken window and said, 'Dave's leading the horses out now, time to get gone,' and he hurried back up the alley way.

The three men in the office moved out after him. Cooper stopped at the corner.

'I'll cover you,' he said.

The street seemed empty but he stood and hoped that someone would show their face. He never regretted killing anyone, he waited with as much conscience as his shadow. He heard the horses' hoofs thump as they crowded into the alley behind him. He emptied his gun into the street and he ran to his horse.

They all mounted apart from Dave Mooney, who stood and held the reins of a tired looking mule with the grain sacks strapped on its back.

'My horse is lame,' he said, 'I had to leave it in the stall.'

'We've got to leave you too, Dave,' said Flem Mooney in a quiet voice, his face still and expressionless like a flat wall. He grabbed the mule reins from his brother. 'You're on your own, find us up at Rogue River in two days.' His eyes filled with spite. 'If you can.'

Fred Cooper leaned forward in his saddle, rested a hand on the pommel, wiped his nose with his coat sleeve and smiled, his pinched face brutal and as tight as a clenched fist.

Dave Mooney spat on the floor and moved back a step as the horses snorted and pitched their heads and stamped their feet with impatience.

He started towards the livery when a rider burst

around the corner of the building, pulled his horse up hard and scrambled for his gun. Chris Stover shot him out of his saddle and he flipped backwards as if someone had yanked him over with an invisible wire. The empty horse tried to run but Stover caught the trailing reins and said, 'Here, Dave, you always played fair by me. Maybes it didn't pan out, but I can't see you left for dead. Mount up right smart.'

Mooney hesitated as they all sat and waited. He gave Stover a withering look then shrugged and vaulted into the saddle.

'Let's ride,' said Flem Mooney and they all booted their horses out into open country.

Fred Cooper had a face like thunder, he desperately wanted to leave Dave Mooney behind, the town folk would rip him apart. Dave brought up the rear and fought to hide his own disappointment. There was nothing wrong with his horse, he just did not want to leave with them. The last thing he wanted was to be was riding out with this lot for company and two sacks full of nothing.

6

As the Mooney gang ran away, Eddie Carter cantered his horse through Oregon Territory towards Sailors Diggings. He felt bone tired as if he had not slept in years. He found that if he twisted slightly in the saddle his wound seemed easier. Now and again he slipped his boots out of the stirrups to ease the pain that throbbed over his left hip. The shock from the shot crept through his body, his left arm shivered and he felt light-headed. He rode his big black Morgan horse and he could feel that he wanted to run; the horse stamped and tossed his head, shaking his mane but Carter held him back and moved smoothly with the sway of the horse's back.

The dusty narrow trail climbed through a steep sided rock canyon, rising to an upland covered in trees and there the country opened out and the land fell away. He realized that he was near Cave Junction and knew he was getting close. He stopped and looked down over the horse's head while he absent-mindedly stroked his ears, he could see there was mining in the hills. He saw footbridges across streams and creeks made of felled logs still covered in bark and moss, large rocks and mining pits with leavings heaped beside them. He noticed tents, make-shift shelters put together from tree boughs covered in old calico shirts, rickety plank hovels and a couple of log cabins.

Carter arrived at Sailors Diggings in the early evening. It lay tucked under a mountain that rose above the buildings and bristled with dark leafed timber. He could smell wet stone and warm dust and saw a long ribbon of water coming down through a funnel of trees but no-one seemed to be working hereabouts. He rode down the main street with people standing around in groups and was surprised at how busy the place seemed. He pulled up in front of a store, tied his horse and walked across to a muddle of locals gathered outside the Rusty Nail saloon. A man stood on a wooden box and talked down to them. He wore a smart brown suit and vest, had shrewd eyes and oiled glossy hair under the rim of his bowler hat. He stood on a box, his spindly legs under a stomach that sagged and bulged like an over-stuffed pillow. His thick solid looking moustache went down the sides of his mouth to his chin. Carter took an instant dislike to him but could not have said why. Meet Horace Crick.

Now Horace did not make his own fortune, his

sort never do, he came into it from his father. His old man was a crook who sold land he didn't own to unsuspecting farmers and fiddled Army supply contracts.

Horace inherited his money ten years ago when he was about twenty. His father fell off a barn roof and broke his neck. That was Horace's story anyway. Folk could never quite see why old Crick would be on a barn roof in the first place but apparently he was and then, accidently it seems, he came crashing down head first. Lucky Horace.

Carter stood on the edge of the crowd and listened to him speak.

'We need all the help we can get,' Crick said. 'We've got over twenty men out there chasing these cold-blooded murderers. I want more of you to join the hunt. Now many of you know me, Horace Crick, as a man of my word.' No-one spoke. 'They stole close to $75,000 worth of gold from my assay office.' A murmur went through those listening. 'Well, let me tell you something – I'm offering a big reward.' He paused and halved the figure he thought of. 'Two thousand dollars to anyone who gets that gold back for me.'

'How many dead are there?' a woman asked.

'Seventeen including two women,' said Crick, bowing his head dramatically. 'We pray for their souls.'

'Who done it?' called another voice.

'Well, there was at least five of them, maybe more,

things aren't too clear as it all happened right quick. Two of the men looked alike – we believe they're brothers, one had a scarred face. Someone reckons they recognized one as a rat called Fred Cooper. That's all we've got.'

He coughed and took his watch out of his vest pocket.

'Now as I say, they rode out not thirty minutes ago and we had men on their trail ten minutes later. I figure we need another group to follow on and help out. They rode northwest to O'Brien.' The men surrounding him began to shout, wave guns and everyone started talking at once.

Carter turned, mounted up and wheeled away out of the settlement. He knew it must be the same gang and his rage grew stronger, his hands trembled and his face clustered with anger. He knew the land a little around O'Brien and he urged his horse on towards it, allowing the Morgan to have a loose rein and the stallion's hoofs hammered against the hard packed earth until his neck and flanks shone dark with sweat and wisps of saliva flew from his mouth. Carter closed in.

Ahead of him, the Mooney gang had galloped hard after they left the settlement and then eased their horses to a steady canter. Flem Mooney still pulled the mule with the sacks on a long rein behind him.

'This mule's winded by the weight of the gold,' he shouted above the drum of the hoofs. 'We need to take it easy for a while. Keep an eye on the back trail.'

They all turned in their saddles but the horizon was clear. After another five minutes Chris Stover hawked the dust from his throat and said, 'How about we split up?'

They all slowed to a walk. Fred Cooper pulled alongside Stover, wiped the sweat off his face with his shirt and said, 'What about the gold? I ain't going nowhere without my cut.'

Miles Horn nodded in agreement.

'Wait,' said Dave Mooney, 'how in the hell are we going to carry our own shares if we split it? There's only two sacks and one mule.' He did not want any of them looking in the sacks. But no-one had an answer anyway so they speeded up and rode on in silence.

A while later Cooper said, 'This goddamn mule ain't making good enough time. If they set off after us they're going to catch us – unless we share the gold out.'

Dave Mooney scowled at Cooper's back, he knew that if they opened the sacks he was in big trouble for sure. He looked around and wondered if he should drop back and ride off and leave them to it; they'd likely let him go but Cooper might just gun him down for the hell of it. He slowed his horse and glanced back down the trail.

'Lookit,' he called, pointing back towards Sailors Diggings. In the distance a cloud of dust snaked over the horizon, a black speck appeared and then others gathered around it like distant flies. In a moment or two they could make out horses and riders, and the thrum of horse hoofs rolled towards them as the riders flowed like liquid down a ridge, pulling up a screen of dirt from the trail.

'We got company all right,' said Flem Mooney. 'Ride hard.'

They galloped on until Chris Stover called, 'They're gaining on us, this load's too goddamn heavy for the mule. They'll be on us in the next hour.'

'Dump the gold, Flem,' shouted Dave Mooney.

'Never. We shot them up good back there, they're only used to grubbing in the ground, they're better with a shovel than a gun. I say we shoot it out. They'll like as run when they see we've got some backbone.'

'Look over yonder,' said Cooper, pointing to a high butte that rose steeply from the flat pasture. It was a hump of land clustered with rock and trees. 'Let's get over there and take the fight to them. We can hold out until nightfall and shoot them up some. They won't have the guts to stay after dark.'

'Let's do it,' said Flem Mooney.

They left the trail and headed for the safety of the rocks.

Eddie Carter heard the gunfire. He rode through a stand of pine up an incline coated with tangled bushes towards the shooting. He remembered that the Illinois River ran in these parts but thought it was further north, and he cut through the rough landscape towards the noise. He topped a ridge and immediately in front of him the land lifted in a deep sided hill that rose to a small plateau. Outcrops of rock jutted from the worn slopes bevelled and scalloped by the wind over time and ponderosa pine grew in scattered clumps across the small flat hill top.

He pulled his horse up, took his field glasses out of their battered green leather case and studied the land. He saw what he figured was the vigilante posse, they surrounded the base of the hill in a scattered circle, hidden behind rocks and trees and shot at the outlaws above them on the high ground.

He saw occasional gun flashes from the top and noticed that two of the gang hid in the trees covering this side. He heard shots from the far side and figured they had spread out to stop anyone climbing up. A deep draw ran down one side and he guessed the Mooneys rode up that way. As he watched, a vigilante rider kicked his horse into a run and tried to scramble up the same draw but a gun flashed from the rocks above it and the boom of a rifle echoed across the plain as the rider toppled from his horse and fell in a dusty heap.

Carter dismounted, pulled his horse forward to a straggling stunted tree, tied the reins off to a low branch and went forward on foot. He took his time, his gaze fixed on the rocks above him. As he neared the foot of the hill, he crawled into a ditch boiling with insects and inched through an untidy lump of bushes into tall rank grass. He sat up, hidden by the undergrowth and loaded his carbine. He took out a paper cartridge, half cocked the rifle, pulled the rifle lever down and slotted the cartridge in with his thumb. He brought the lever back and watched the breech cut the paper end of the cartridge off. With the firing cap ready, he could see the gunpowder and felt confident it would fire.

He looked up when he heard movement to his left and he watched a vigilante stand and race over to a tree at the base of the gradient. Carter glanced up and one of the outlaws rose up from the cover of the rocks and fired two quick shots with a handgun. The second shot caught the vigilante in the shoulder and he cried out and hunkered down behind the tree trunk. Carter raised his carbine, pulled the hammer back to full cock, tucked the stock into his shoulder and waited. He felt the warm smooth wood of the stock against his cheek as he sighted down the barrel at the rock where the gang member last showed himself. Then he patiently waited for him to break cover. The wounded vigilante pulled himself to his feet and tried to run back to safety and as soon as he set off, the gunman stood and Carter had a clear view of his tall thin silhouette. He squeezed the trigger and the heavy bullet whacked the gunman in the chest and he toppled like a felled tree back into the rocks.

'Miles,' he heard another outlaw call from off to the left but Miles could not answer, for he was dead.

Carter knew that he needed to get to the top of the hill. The Mooneys were trapped but in the stand-off, the vigilantes were getting picked off while they figured out what to do. Carter realized that if the outlaws held out until dark they could break out and disappear in the night. He decided that the only clear gap lay just above him where he had just shot the one called Miles.

Take it to them, he said to himself, don't think about it; just get it done. It's time to kill them all deader than hell. He crept forward, sliding like the shadow of a mountain lion and closed in on the hill-side and the Mooneys.

Two vigilantes saw Carter come out of the grass and start to climb.

'Who's that?'

'I don't know, Walt, I cain't see his face. Besides which, there's a lot of folk with us that we ain't never seen afore. I hear there's hundreds of placers mining at the Diggings and we got a real mix of them out here looking. All I know is he's going up the hill so he must be with us. I bet he's the feller who just shot one of them deader than a door nail.'

'Let's give him some covering fire, there's one of the gunmen over by that tree yonder stopping us from riding up that draw.'

'Right, make sure you fire well away from the feller climbing though, we don't want to hit him.'

'When was the last time you hit anything, Walt?'

The two men started shooting and kept up a slow deliberate volley of fire until they saw Carter reach the top and disappear into the rocks. The two vigi-lantes reloaded and waited.

Carter rolled into a cleft between two rocks. He sat and listened with the heat from the rock on his back and the hot smell of warm stone around him. The sweat coursed down his ribs. He pressed a hand to his side, he felt blood leaking from the hip wound, the dampness on his fingers and thigh. He shrugged his shoulders, the belt felt tight and he could do nothing about it now. He reloaded his carbine, the stock gleamed and he could smell the tallow that he had rubbed in to it the week before. He took his hat off, glanced over a boulder and looked for his next shot.

He scanned the ground, looking for the gunman covering the entrance to the plateau. If he cleared the way the vigilantes could ride up and finish the job.

The grass and undergrowth rippled in the light breeze and he saw a huge slab of rock by the opening to the draw. He caught sight of a red shirt in the shade of the boulder. As he watched the man shift position and half turn, Carter recognized the big man with the drooping moustache as one of the brothers from the morning attack. He remembered the murder of his friend Nate and the anger welled up in his throat but he fought for control and calm before his shot. He rested his elbows on the rock in front of him, pulled the metal butt plate of the rifle into his shoulder, focused down the iron sights and squeezed the trigger. He watched the dust puff up from the gunman's shirt and nailed him in the side of the chest. The impact knocked Flem Mooney forward like he had been clubbed from behind with a giant hammer and he rolled down the rocks to the bottom of the hill. A shout of triumph went up from the watching vigilantes when they saw him fall.

Carter reloaded and looked across the small plateau. He noticed Fred Cooper, recognized him immediately and recalled his name and how he killed his friend in cold blood. Cooper stood about forty paces away and their eyes locked across the clearing. Cooper raised his gun but Carter threw a shot off first. The bullet caught Cooper's gun hand, blew off his thumb and hurled his gun into the air. Cooper reeled back a pace, sat down hard and clamped his mangled hand under his other arm.

'That's for Nate,' whispered Carter but everything jacked out of focus, the energy seemed to drain from his body and his own loss of blood forced him to sit. Spots swam before his eyes and his head felt like it was drifting off his shoulders. He passed out.

Carter had killed two of the outlaws, Flem Mooney and Miles Horn, and he had wounded Fred Cooper. While Carter lay unconscious, a bunch of vigilantes rode up the unguarded draw onto the hilltop, looking to ring the last drop of blood out of the murderers that shot up Sailors Diggings.

A vigilante raced a big Dun horse across the plateau. He slapped it across the rump with his hat and bolted for the far side of the hill. Chris Stover jumped up from behind a bush, shouted and waved his arms to spook the horse as he tried to drag the rider from the saddle. The horse veered sideways but the rider hung on and, as he passed Stover, he drew a gun, turned in the saddle and shot Stover in the knee. Stover grunted, his long legs crumpled under him, his wounded leg twisted awkwardly. He pushed himself back to his feet and raised his rifle to his shoulder. A second rider came straight at him from behind and trampled his thin body into the dust. Five more riders circled him and they sat on their horses and shot Stover, shredding his carcass to a bloody pulp. It looked like there was not enough of him left to fill a bucket. Someone shouted, 'Well, if you have to kill a feller you might as well kill him once and for all.'

7

Dave Mooney left. He saw the others being picked off one at a time and he slithered through the rocks and made his way down the opposite side of the butte. Grit slid under his boots and dust rose into his face. Below him the hillside dropped steeply, thick with trees and streaked with shadow, the air alive with noise, the tree branches creaked and the wind rustled the foliage. As the land levelled off he swished his way through grass that felt dry and stiff against his legs.

Now Dave Mooney thought himself a lucky man and he trusted his luck. As he came down off the hill he looked around and could not see anyone. His head ached and he could taste the whiskey they drank in town and his tongue felt like leather. He could smell the hot arid air. The sun seemed so bright that the whole sky shone. Still, he reckoned he wasn't doing too badly considering the afternoon he'd had.

He recalled the simple plan that came to him while he waited in the assay office. He felt mad as hell when the others told him they did not want to ride with him anymore but he let the fury simmer while he chewed over how he would make them pay. Well, he'd show them, they'd stepped on a rattler's tail when they riled him. The assay office was loaded with gold and he was the goddamn buck to take it. Even better, he'd get his dumb brother and the other beef-heads to help him rob the office. Then he could let them lead any posse away while he rode off in the other direction, alone and rich.

He remembered the satisfaction he felt when he filled two sacks with rocks and dust, tied them to a mule and brought them out with the horses for the others. He left the gold in his horse stall covered in straw. He knew they'd believe him when he said his horse was lame and he could have laughed out loud when they made it obvious that they just wanted rid of him. He was so close then, all he had to do was let the townsfolk chase them out of town while he hid until dark and then he could load up the gold and ride away.

Then that fool Chris Stover found him a ride and he had to leave with them, eating their trail dust and following a mule loaded with stone and dirt. He smiled, it all came right in the end. They were all dead and he was free, he just needed to find a horse, ride back and get the gold from where he hid it at the livery. His headache eased.

He walked down a dry gulch, careless of the noise he made; the gravel crunched under his boots. As he looked back over his shoulder a man stepped out of the shadows and spoke, startling Mooney.

'Hold it right there, mister,' he said. He held an old Remington Mississippi rifle pointed at Mooney's stomach. He was a tall, stooped miner with a square chin, big bones in his cheeks, the skin stretched tight across them. He wore his hat on the side of his head and long strings of lank hair hung over his face. Mooney saw his chest rise and fall as he stood in front of him. They could hear shots on the hill above them as the man stepped forward.

'What's going on up there?' He clearly thought that Mooney was one of the vigilantes.

Mooney stepped across, grabbed the gun barrel and wrenched the gun away from the miner. He put both hands on the barrel and smashed the rifle stock into the vigilante's stomach. As he fell to his knees, Mooney brought his knee up into the side of his face then picked a hunk of rock up and crushed his head.

He pulled the dead man's gun out of his belt and straightened up. He heard a horse snort and a man cough. He grabbed the dead body and carried it behind a high wedge of rock. A creek ran out behind the rocks, the cool air in the glade felt damp and smelled of wet earth. He saw a half submerged dead tree with a thick green trunk shining in the light through the canopy of trees. He tossed the body into the undergrowth behind it, wiped a streak of mud down his cheek to hide his scar, pulled his hat down and edged back around the rock. As he stepped out, he surprised two vigilantes who walked past leading their horses. They saw Mooney and swung their guns up and eyed him with suspicion.

Mooney glanced at them, confident he could kill them both even though he had not drawn his gun, but he had a better, quieter idea. He put his finger to his lips for silence and nodded hello. He waved them away from the rocks and whispered, 'I think there's one of them behind those rocks. I reckon he's trying to make a run for it. I'm going to take a look, you two wait here and cover me. You hear me on that, I need you to watch my back. Stay put.'

The two men looked at each other and one of them shrugged and nodded. Mooney disappeared from sight, ran to the creek bed and yanked the dead miner out. He carried the body back over his shoulder to the waiting vigilantes. He kept his gun in his hand in case they recognized the dead miner but his luck held; they barely glanced at the body. Mooney said, 'I saved some lead and stove his head in.'

One of them clapped Mooney on the shoulders while the other stomped on the dead man's legs when Mooney tossed the body onto the ground.

'Right, partners,' said Mooney, 'you get this one up top with the others. I'll get my horse and follow you.' He walked off without giving them the chance to reply or consider what had happened. He passed their horses, the Dun swished her tail and the chestnut next to it shivered across the flanks, he resisted the temptation to take them and run for it. He turned to see the two men watching him so he ran a hand down the chestnut's flank and patted the rump as he moved out of sight.

A couple of minutes later he found a mule that stood belly deep in the grass tethered to a bush. The mule stopped eating and looked up.

'Time to move out, I've got my gold to collect,' said Mooney. He moved off at walking pace, guessing that a walking mule attracted less attention than a galloping one. He was glad that the rest of the gang were dead.

He was wrong on that count.

8

Fred Cooper was still going. His right thumb had been shot clean away but he dragged the bandana from his neck and bound his hand, knotting it at the wrist and pulling the cloth tight with his teeth.

He'd been hurt before and made it out. He reckoned he still had a lick of life left in him yet. He recalled the last time he'd been hurt bad he rode with Warren Allen. Back then they lived in an old house in Dimmit County. About ten of them, vicious work that suited him, they stole ranch horses or cattle and robbed corn cribs. They killed if they could get away with it. One morning they'd stolen a herd of cattle from six Mexican vaqueros near Eagle Pass and killed them all. When they got back, they sat playing poker under a shed-like extension in front of their cabin when twenty or so Texas Rangers rode in hard. They'd all jumped up and started for the house to get their guns but the rangers killed half of them before they got inside the door. Cooper ran through the cabin, dived through a back window and ran hell for leather across to the woods. They shot him twice in the back. He rolled down a wide arroyo but no-one followed him, they left him for dead. He dragged himself away and lived off sour berries and squirrel, when he was lucky. But he'd come through it right enough and sworn then that whatever he'd done bad before was nothing to what he would do next. He reckoned he'd lived up to that promise.

He looked down at his mangled hand and tried not to think about the agony that flared up his arm, he told himself that pain was just the other side of feeling good and almost believed it. He figured if he made it to the rocks behind him he could get clean away. He never made the rocks though.

Don Plunkett, a tough looking miner with a wild beard, big meaty shoulders and a good natured face that normally shone as warm as a sunny day dragged Cooper into the centre of the plateau like a sack of feed. He could barely contain his anger, he had broad hands laced with scars and he gripped Cooper by his throat and, one handed, lifted him to his feet and slammed his back against a tree trunk.

'One of you shot my brother back there, there's going to be a reckoning. You're a coward and men like you are ten a cent, you ain't worth spit.'

'I hear that a lot, it don't bother me none,' said Cooper, his face purple with lack of air. 'I ain't afraid of dying neither.'

'No,' said Plunkett, 'it's living that the likes of you

cain't handle.'

Don Plunkett was the son of a god fearing revivalist preacher who could see a sin forming in young Don's mind and would whip the wickedness from his soul to save him from an eternity of everlasting fire. Don left home at thirteen, his brother went with him. At fifteen, Don beat a champion free-for-all wrestler from out East who tried bullying him in a store. After that he just seemed to get tougher.

The vigilantes gathered the dead bodies together, dragged them to a level sandy clearing just off to the side of where Cooper stood pinned to the tree. Tension gripped them, they worked closely together in silence but all of them knew that the killing had not finished yet, they eyed Cooper and let their anger build. They picked a big old thick trunked oak, it stood like black metal against the sun with piles of dead leaves like graves around the base and among the widespread roots.

Someone called across to Don Plunkett.

'Don, you ease off on his throat now, we don't want you choking the life out of him before we swing him proper.'

Cooper felt the stranglehold ease but the blood still sang in his ears and he could hear his own hoarse breathing. Well, he thought, this is it. Still and all, I bet if they'd seen what I've seen and lived the life I've had they wouldn't be no different to me. I'll be damned if I don't go down hard, whatever they do to me.

The vigilantes gathered around Cooper like a fist, a red-haired man who looked as thin and rough skinned as a yellow-legged frog stepped forward, looking hard at Cooper. He paused and glanced around the group. He scowled and then the scowl turned into a hollow smile.

'My name's Melvin Priddy. I work for the man you stole the gold from, he's called Mr Crick and he wants his gold back. Most of these others lost family or friends back there. You killed upwards of seventeen decent folk. What in the hell did you do that for?'

Fred Cooper looked him in the eye, shrugged his shoulders and said, 'I reckon because killing people's easier than it should be. I don't know why you're surprised about it, that's why we all carry guns, ain't it? Killing makes me feel good, there ain't nothing complicated about it. Even if you kill me it don't mean I'm going to change.'

'Come on,' someone called out to the red-haired man, 'let's get to it.'

'What's your name?' said Priddy to Cooper.

'I'm Fred Cooper,' Cooper spoke with pride. 'Maybe you heard of me.' He turned his head as far as he could with the hand still gripping his throat and he looked down at the bodies. 'The skinny feller you shot up good is Chris Stover, the one with the moustache is Flem Mooney and the ugly one next to him is Miles Horn.' Suddenly Cooper's face flushed with rage and he banged his own head back against the tree, an evil light in his eyes and said, 'Goddamn it, God damn you, Dave Mooney.' His hoarse voice grated like a shovel across stone. 'You stupid fools. There's one of us missing and it's the only one I wanted dead. Dave Mooney.'

The vigilantes all looked from Cooper to the bodies laid in the dirt.

'So who's the other body we've got here then?' said Priddy. His confusion building into fury, he looked around at the other miners and people from the settlement. 'Maybe there was more than five of them?'

Cooper called out, flecks of spit on his lips and strings of saliva running down his chin, 'That other body ain't one of us, you idiot. You're looking for Dave Mooney, a big man with a scarred, torn face.'

A small man stepped forward and looked down at the last body.

'You know I think I recognize that feller, he's one of us right enough. I don't know his name but he's a placer, I think he's up on that far ridge that looks down onto Esterly Lakes. He must have rode out with us to help out.'

Priddy whirled around and stood with his hands on his hips.

'Which durned fool brought that body up?' he said.

A man stepped forward, he hawked a gob of tobacco juice into the dust.

'We did,' he nodded to a second man beside him,

'and I don't take kindly to being called a fool. Especially not by a jumped up runt like you, Melvin "Yes Mr Crick' Priddy or whatever your name was.' He moved forward, stood up close, stared at Priddy and forced him to look away.

Priddy's jaw tightened, he swallowed and in a quiet voice he said, 'Well, what the heck happened?'

'We was at the bottom of the hill over yonder when a feller said he'd seen one of the gang behind a rock. He went over and he came back out and said he'd like as stove his head in. We collected the body and brought it up here.' He looked at the body then up at his friend, shrugged and said, 'How was we to know? We don't know half the folk riding with us, none of us do I guess. The feller who shot him was a big man with a dark muddy beard and a ripped face for sure.'

Priddy made to say something but he saw the man in front of him clench his fist and stare at him with a look that could burn paint off wood. Priddy thought better of it and looked around. He ran his fingers up his throat and across his chin.

'Right, we need to find this Mooney. First off we need to round up their horses. We got the mule and the sacks tethered back there, we'd best take the bodies back and start over. Fetch a rope somebody,' said Priddy, turning back to look at Fred Cooper. 'Let's string this one up and get back to Sailors Diggings.'

Don Plunkett, the big miner holding Cooper by

the throat, turned and scowled at Priddy.

'Hey, Priddy, you're riling me right quick. Don't you go telling us how to do this, you're only here because your boss Crick lost his gold. We're here to get justice for the folks who was shot. So you take your peckerwood face and your shiny suit and you back off a mite.'

Priddy fiddled with the belt buckle on his trousers, his gaze fixed on the ground at his feet, his sullen face seemed to say that he knew tomorrow would only be worse than today.

'Have it your way, Plunkett, you know I've got a job to do is all. And quit going on about my suit, at least I don't look like I was rope drug through brambles like you do.' Before Plunkett could react Priddy said, 'Let's get to the hanging.'

Everyone started to move. In an angry surge of noise they crowded in, a vigilante flicked a rope over a high branch and two men picked up the trailing end. Priddy moved forward, holding the noose ready to loop over Cooper's head. Cooper wriggled and began to snap his teeth and spit like a cornered lynx. Plunkett still held Cooper pinned to the tree, he backhanded him across the face, forcing Cooper's head sideways and drawing blood across his cheek. Plunkett took the rope off Priddy, looped it over Cooper's head and drew it tight.

'Lift,' he said and two men hauled on the rope, stretching Cooper's neck until his toes barely touched the ground.

'Hey, Priddy,' someone called. 'Lookit. The bags on this mule are filled with trail dirt, rock and horse dung, there ain't no gold.'

The two men heaved on the rope and lifted Cooper off his feet and his last thoughts were that not only had Dave Mooney escaped but he'd got the gold away as well. The idea hit him like a nail in the skull as they choked the life out of him. The thought that Mooney got away with it hurt him more than the hanging.

Cooper fought them like a wild cat, he bucked and twisted as they dragged the breath out of him, they yanked his writhing body up and down a few times, jiggling him in the air and hauling on his feet until, finally, he stopped moving. He dangled from the bough of the tree on a green-leafed gallows like an old puppet made of rags. They let him drop and ran over to the mule to see what all the commotion was about. Plunkett and a couple of others showed less interest in the gold than the rest. He checked Cooper was dead, he saw his face streaked with blood and his neck as stiff as a chunk of pipe. He looked like he had been shot out of a cannon, maybe more than once. Plunkett spat in Cooper's face.

'That's for my brother. This world's a better place without you and your kind.' He hefted him onto his shoulder like a side of beef and walked over to the others.

9

Above them in the rocks Eddie Carter opened his eyes. He lay on his back, looked up at the sky and for a moment he could not think where he was. He felt light headed and weak and as the pain from his side seeped up across his back, he remembered. He pushed himself to his feet and leaned against a rock while his head cleared. He heard raised voices and saw the vigilantes grouped on the plateau down below him. A movement in the corner of his eye made him turn and he saw a lone rider walking a mule across country in the direction of Sailors Diggings. Carter realized that apart from the lone rider, all of the vigilantes had gathered on the top of the hill. He saw five bodies laid across the backs of horses and the vigilantes stood around a mule. A red-haired man shouted above the others and waved his arms about, Carter heard him talk to the group.

'Listen, will you? Stop kicking, this arguing ain't getting us anywhere. The gold ain't here. Like as not they've hidden it, buried maybe and filled the sacks with rubbish to fool us.'

'Well, Priddy, we cain't ask them seeing as how they're all dead,' said a thin man, sweeping his arm behind him to the bodies on the horses.

'No, you heard what that hayseed called Cooper said before we hanged him, he said that Dave Mooney is still alive. We've got to find him, he'll know where the gold is.'

'When we saw him he was at the bottom of the hill, he could be anywhere by now.'

Priddy held his hands up for quiet and said, 'It's getting on for dusk. We need to search the top of this hill before dark and make sure that the gold ain't buried or hidden in the rocks. Remember the reward. I say we spread out in a line and walk across north to south, we're looking for fresh dirt or sacks wedged in the gaps between rocks. I don't reckon they had time to hide it while we was chasing them, it must be up here. We'll have a look before we go back and tell the others what's happened.' He turned and shouted, 'Henderson, mount up and ride to Sailors Diggings, you tell them we lost four men but killed four of them. At least one got away. He's called Dave Mooney, he's big and ugly with a scarred face.'

A placer mounted up.

'You'd better tell them the gold ain't here. We're staying until dark looking for Mooney and the gold. Tell them to get more folk out here to help us.'

They did not notice Carter up in the rocks and he decided to leave them to it. He slipped away back down the hill to find his horse. He had no interest in the gold but he saw and heard that four of them were dead and that thought pleased him, especially Fred Cooper dying. He had to find Dave Mooney though. He mounted up, confident the rider he saw calmly walking off earlier must be Mooney, who else could it be? He reckoned Mooney would risk everything for the gold and the only reason that Mooney headed back towards Sailors Diggings was because the gold was there, maybe it had never left the settlement.

While the vigilantes searched the hill outside of O'Brien, Eddie Carter followed Dave Mooney back to Sailors Diggings.

Mooney had a head start. He did not know that Carter saw him making his solitary way back to Sailors Diggings; all that Mooney thought about was the gold. All Carter could think about was his friend Nate Hollingsworth and about bringing justice head on to Dave Mooney. He rode with his hand on his gun, determined to face him down and see who walked away.

10

As Carter arrived back at Sailors Diggings, the sky was still light but the dark filled the valley floor, the settlement laid under a bowl of shadow. The glow from the lamps in the buildings spilled out in a shower of light across the low ground. The settlement was not much more than a large dirt crossroads. Torn shreds of cloud swirled over the treetops as he looked down to the livery on the edge of town. The back doors stood open and the brassy light from inside silhouetted a small figure raking out the stables. Carter closed in and saw it was a young boy clearing the yard. The boy looked up but carried on working while Carter sat on his horse and watched. He leaned forward and bent over the saddle horn.

'Howdy,' Carter said. The boy wiped an arm across his forehead and nodded. 'I'm new in these parts, I work a claim in Patrick Creek California if you know it.'

'I've heard of it,' said the boy.

Carter dismounted and walked over, held out his hand and said, 'I'm Eddie Carter.'

'I'm Floyd Kindersley.' The boy smiled and shook his hand.

'You own this livery, Floyd?' said Carter, grinning.

'No, sir, my grandpa does but I work here right enough. Fine horse you got there, a Morgan like that can run all day if he's grain fed.'

'You sure know your horses, Floyd. Can you give him some grain while me and you talk? Here's a dollar, you keep that for yourself, you hear me on that?'

Carter needed information and thought that Floyd would be able to tell him what had happened at the stables during the day. He sat on an upturned barrel, picked a piece of straw out of a bale, stuck it in his mouth and watched Floyd see to his horse. He brought out a bucket and set it in front of the Morgan.

'There ain't too much in there, we'll let him help himself,' said Floyd and he started to brush the horse down; the horse's sleek black coat shone in the lamp-light.

'Floyd, I'm looking for a feller, he's a mean one, big with a scarred face and a black beard. Have you seen him today?'

'Have I,' said Floyd with feeling. 'He was in here not an hour ago, he's as ugly as a mud fence. Hit me for nothing. You going to kill him I hope.'

'Tell me what happened.' Carter needed to get

moving but thought it better to sit a while, no point pushing him, he'd learn more if he let the youngster have his say.

'Well, he was in here this afternoon. I heard him telling those others that his horse was lame but he was lying like a rug, the horse was right as rain. I cleaned the stall out and I'm telling you that horse was fine. Anyhow he left the horse here and lit out this afternoon, took one of our mules. He left two grain sacks under the straw in the stall corner, I tried to move them but they was so heavy. I just let them be and cleaned around as best I could. Well, he came back tonight, like I said, and give me a whaling, said I'd been looking to steal from him. I told him straight I hadn't touched his dadburned sacks. He grumbled and cussed but loaded another mule he'd hired from us this morning and rode out. He went on the horse, he said was lame when it wasn't. Don't that beat all?'

Carter leaned forward and put his hands on his knees.

'You know what, Floyd, I reckon that feller's cleverer than he looks. Him and his gang shot up your town today and stole a pile of gold. Before they ran off, he hid the gold in your livery and came back tonight to collect it. I bet he double crossed the rest of the gang, they all thought they was toting the gold when they rode out just like everyone else did. The rest of them's dead now anyway so he's got the gold to himself.'

'You mean those bags he hid in the stall were full of gold?' Floyd said and whistled.

'Yes, sir,' said Carter. 'I hear they killed more than seventeen people and stole over $75,000 worth of gold today. Men like that deserve to die so that the rest of us can get on with our lives.' He closed his eyes and took a deep breath and when he opened them again he said, 'They killed my partner this morning.'

He grunted as he stood and pushed his hand against his wound. 'Shot me in the back. Look, I'd best get moving, Floyd. I'm not a man who looks for trouble but I fight when I have to fight and kill when I have to kill. I killed two men today and like as killed a third. I hope to kill another one yet. I'm going to find the man with the scarred face and make him pay. After that I hope to get a little peace, I reckon by then I won't owe nobody nothing.'

Floyd led his horse over and said in wonder, 'Seventy-five thousand dollars.'

Carter raised a finger.

'Seventeen dead, son, that's what we should remember first.'

They both turned when they heard the scrape of boots on the livery floor and a man in his fifties stood silhouetted in the doorway. He shone with sweat, he wiped his face with an old shirt. He had a long narrow face with a high forehead and thinning dark hair. He wore strap overalls but no shirt because of the heat from the blacksmith forge, his muscles on his arms looked stretched and stringy with age. The sweat clung to his body like a coat of cream. He nodded towards Carter.

'Evening. I'm Floyd's grandpa, Bill Kindersley, but everyone calls me Grandpa. I heard what you said. I got back in not long ago, I've been helping folk bury their dead. It's hard to believe they could have done what they did. Did you say some of the killers are dead?'

'They are that, I shot two of them myself. The riders from here killed another and strung a fourth up.'

Grandpa Kindersley lit up a pipe, holding a match to the bowl until the smoke wreathed his head. He coughed and his lungs crackled with phlegm. He walked across to his grandson Floyd and put an arm around his shoulders and said to Carter, 'You be right careful, mister, he'll kill you and think nothing of it, we've seen what him and his kind can do. They bring a bit of darkness with them wherever they go.'

Carter had nothing to say, it did not matter what anyone said to him; he intended to go after Mooney even if he had to ride into Hell.

He mounted up, stretched forward and patted the horse's strong neck, pushed his hat up on his brow with his fingers and said, 'Which way did he go, Floyd?'

Floyd pointed.

'East. The horse and mule need at least five gallons of water a day each so he'll have to get to the east fork of the Illinois River by morning. Then he'll have to stay with the river until he gets to Takilma. Leastways that's what I done told him when he left.'

'Floyd, I bet you're the smartest huckleberry in this here territory. Have you told anyone else what you know?'

Floyd studied Carter and liked him, his calmness was part of it but there was something else, he just knew when he set his mind to anything he'd get it done.

'No, sir, I've only told you, he threatened to come back and get me proper if I said anything so I kept quiet. But I've told you because I reckon if you're on his tail then he ain't coming back.'

11

Carter headed east. His shadow stretched before him, his silhouette haloed with the sun's last red light. He rode on through the dusk as single stars appeared and glittered in a grey sky. Carter felt angry and impatient but he went at the same steady canter, always on the lookout, checking his back trail and his eyes sweeping the land. The night closed in and took the colour out of everything, matching his dark mood. The scent of the trees strengthened with the darkness.

Later he passed into a trough of land, the sides thick with trees that thinned as the trail climbed to the ridge, from there the land opened up and fell away in a wide sweep. The trail sloped downwards, steeply at first but flattened out into a jumble of rocks scattered with red cedar trees and clumps of spruce.

His horse raised his head and snorted. Carter wondered if he had smelt water so he reined him in and stood still, staring into the night, listening. He opened his mouth to hear better and as he breathed in, he caught the faint aroma of coffee boiling and pork frying.

The smell took him back to a memory from four years ago that he recalled as clearly as yesterday. It had been early morning, he paddled his canoe up a small creek to take in some traps, rounded a bend and through the mist he saw over thirty Tolowa Indians lining both banks. They dragged him out of the water and took him out onto the prairie. An old warrior told him that they would give him a head start then try and run him down before he got to the Wenaha River. If they caught him they would kill him. Cactus and bunch grass covered the plain that stretched away in front of them as featureless as a rolling ocean.

Carter ran for his life straight across the open prairie, he heard the warriors' whoop and knew the chase was on. He reckoned he ran over three miles before he dared to glance back and to his surprise, he saw that he ran well ahead of them, with the exception of one young brave who raced along with a spear not more than a hundred yards behind him. Carter hurried on, he adjusted his pace to a steady lope that eased his ragged breathing and the fire in his lungs. He ran to within a mile of the river before he heard footsteps closing in. He took a quick look over his shoulder and saw the young Tolowa just behind him, a flume of dust showed that the others were still some way back.

Carter stopped suddenly and turned. He caught the youngster by surprise, and he stumbled and tried to throw his spear but Carter lunged at him, clipped him with a punch on the side of the jaw that rattled his head and he went down and out like a light. He looked so young that Carter could not kill him, instead he broke the spear across his knee, laid the two halves across the youngster's chest and ran on with the other Indians howling and shouting behind him. He made it to the shelter of a heavy thicket of bigleaf maple along the edge of the river. The water ran high on the green sloping banks, he plunged in and the strong current swept him away and left the Indians watching in disbelief. He dragged himself out ten miles lower down, alone in the wilderness without a weapon or horse. It took him two days to walk to the nearest trading post, he arrived sunburned and starving. As he staggered in, the aroma of coffee and frying bacon rushed up to meet him, the smell seemed to grab his face, squeeze his nose and throat and he almost cried out with joy.

So he knew coffee and pork when he smelt it, no matter how faint the scent of it.

Right, he thought, it might not be Mooney but I'll go in expecting him. The breeze is coming up the trail so he's down in those trees, at least that's where I'd camp, the trees and rocks will hide the light from the fire. Mind you, I wouldn't risk a fire or cooking but that doesn't mean he wouldn't.

Carter led his horse off the trail, hobbled him and

moved down the hill. He stood straining his eyes trying to see through the dark shadows cast by a thick screen of trees, but whatever secrets they hid they kept to themselves. He edged through the timber, his carbine in his hand. Walking with care he moved with the breeze, like the wind breathing through the undergrowth. He saw the fire like an orange hole burned in the darkness. Then he saw Mooney next to it, he felt sure it was him even in the poor light. He sat by a deep fire pit and as Carter watched, he tossed a rotted hunk of ponderosa on the fire. He leaned back from the flames and heat as a shower of sparks blew upwards. The firelight lit the side of Mooney's face, streaked his skin red and made his eye a dark hollow. The glow of the fire threw tall shadows on the rocks next to him.

Carter brought his rifle to his shoulder, he curled his finger round the trigger and willed himself to pull it but could not find it himself to shoot a man in the back, even someone like Mooney, even while his anger screamed at him to do it. Instead he said, 'I'll kill you if you move, put your hands high and do it now or I'll pull the trigger.'

He pulled the hammer back. Mooney raised his hands and rested them on his hat. He turned slightly towards the sound of the voice but all he could see was deep black shadow as the man moved towards him. The moonlight silvered the barrel of his rifle and his dark figure emerged, walking with a calm confidence. He finally appeared out of the inky shadows into the light of the fire and Mooney looked into his burning eyes.

Carter said, 'Use your fingertips and toss both guns away from you, left hand first, stay sitting while you do it.' The guns landed with dusty thuds.

Mooney said, 'Right, mister, I done what you asked, now how about telling me what the hell is going on and hurry up about it, my food's getting cold.'

'Remember me?' said Carter. Mooney looked hard at Carter but swung his head back towards the fire.

'Nope,' he said.

'You just don't care, do you? You don't give two nothings about shooting anyone.'

Mooney glanced back over his shoulder.

'Killing's what I do.'

'You hit my claim this morning, don't you remember killing a man and shooting another in the back?'

'You don't say. You must be the one I shot in the back then,' said Mooney.

Carter felt furious, he watched Mooney's face for some emotion but he might as well have been looking at a boulder.

Mooney said, 'Stop fooling around, will you? If you was going to shoot me you'd have done it by now.'

His words hurt like shards of glass in Carter's mind because he knew they were true. He rushed forward and rammed his rifle butt as hard as he could into Mooney's thick neck and Mooney slumped sideways. Carter stumbled, spots swam before his eyes and his head felt as light as a balloon. The floor rushed towards him and he blacked out as exhaustion, hunger and blood loss from the wound in his back drained the strength out of him.

When Carter woke up and opened his eyes, he could smell dirt and wood smoke, the only sound the crackle of the fire next to him. He sat up, Mooney still lay unconscious by his side. Carter lurched to his feet and checked the hammer lock on his rifle was not clogged, then he set it down and poured a coffee from the pot on the fire embers. He found the plate with Mooney's food on it, the fat congealed in a thick layer and the cold bacon stuck to the plate. He picked a hunk of bread up off the ground and brushed the dirt off on his shirt. He pulled the bacon out with his fingers and ate it quickly then he scooped the cold fat up with the dry bread and crammed it in his mouth, wiped his fingers down his shirt and swilled the food down with the hot black coffee. As he drank a second coffee, he watched the sky lighten with the blue glow of the early dawn as the last stars shimmered and faded above him. Mooney stirred, rolled on his back and grunted as he sat up.

'Nobody move,' said a voice. Five men walked in holding rifles at their hips, one of them whistled and two horsemen cantered their horses in.

'You boys been sleeping like you ain't got a care in the world, we got here just before first light and watched you,' said one of the men.

The two horsemen were Horace Crick, the owner of the assay office and the red-headed man who worked for him, Melvin Priddy. Carter recognized one of the riflemen on foot as the big vigilante Don Plunkett who helped hang Cooper the day before.

Melvin Priddy dismounted, walked across to Mooney, stood in front of him with his hands on his hips and said, 'You're Dave Mooney.'

'And you're as ugly as a burnt boot,' said Mooney.

Priddy turned to one of the men and said, 'Is this the man you saw at the bottom of the hill at O'Brien, him that said he'd shot one of the outlaws and left you to deliver the body?'

'That's him all right. He tried to hide the scar but you don't see a face like that and forget it.'

Mooney smiled.

Horace Crick dug his heels into his horse's stomach and walked it across the clearing. His pot belly rolled with the horse's movements, he looked like a sack of potatoes. He came out from the settlement when the vigilantes brought the bodies in and told him they could not find the gold. His florid face looked fit to burst.

'My name is Horace Crick, you stole my gold.'

Carter was not the only one to take an instant dislike to Crick. Everyone sensed there was something about him that was hard to like but it was difficult to say what it was. Folk did not think about it, they just understood that they could not stand him. Crick accepted their hostility, he put it down to jealousy –

he was rich and they were not. He always reckoned there was more to life than being happy anyway.

Crick said, 'I want my gold back, I don't like it when folk steal from me.'

'I didn't ask you to like it,' said Mooney. His eyes looked savage and aggressive but held no fear.

Crick kept his gaze fixed on Mooney's face, scratched his moustache and said,

'We've been looking for you. The other men in your gang are dead, I expect you know that. We searched the hill where we killed them but couldn't find the gold. My guess is that you ran off with it or hid it somewhere along the way. We rode all night looking for you.' Crick looked at Eddie Carter like he was something off the bottom of a hog trough and said to him, 'We didn't realize there were two of you, I guess that would explain why we couldn't find the gold. I figure that you had it all along.'

Carter looked at him and raised his eyebrows in astonishment.

'Now hold on a minute, mister, I ain't with him. I'm Eddie Carter. Fact is it was me that caught him. I've been chasing him since yesterday when they killed my partner down in Patrick Creek and he shot me in the back.'

Melvin Priddy snorted and stepped forward.

'That don't seem likely, it looked to us like you were set here eating and drinking coffee like old friends. You cain't expect us to swallow that story. You're in it with him, that's obvious. Maybe you are from Patrick Creek but that sure would explain a lot. See, that's the trouble with you California boys, you think we're all born stupid up here in Oregon.'

Carter frowned, shook his head and said, 'I was born in Wheatland, Yamhill County, Oregon, about 250 miles north of here.'

'Yes, I bet you was. California folk are all liars as well, we all know that for a goddamn fact.'

Carter pulled up his shirt and showed them the blood stained bandage around his waist.

'Look, I was shot yesterday.'

'There was a lot of people hurt yesterday, mister,' said Priddy. 'All that shows is that one of our boys plugged you good when you shot up the settlement.'

Mooney suppressed a smile, he studied Crick and recognized his type; it was all about the money. He said, 'You, Crick, listen good. The gold's hidden away where you'll never find it. You're a businessman so here's the deal. I'll give you half of it if you let me have the other half and ride away.'

Crick weighed him up with staring lidless reptile eyes and said, 'I'll give you ten thousand.'

The vigilantes murmured in anger.

'Now you hold your goddamn horses there, Crick,' said Don Plunkett in a gritty voice. 'They killed a lot of folk we knew. We got the others that done it and this one dies as well, there ain't any of them riding away from this, you hear me good on that.'

Don Plunkett looked like the kind of man you listened to. He had a hard look about him, as if his shirt was packed with stones, and his sleeves were rolled up on thick sunburned arms. He came across as decent and honest. People saw the scars on his hands but not those that criss-crossed his back and shoulders. Two years ago he'd been hard rock mining, and they sank shafts into solid rock working with picks and shovels. They supported the shafts and tunnels with timber beams along the walls and headframes. They'd hit an underground river and it tore through the tunnel. The torrent swept the two miners in front of Plunkett off their feet but Plunkett grabbed them as they passed and pushed his way across to a side tunnel. The water swept rocks and debris against his back, tearing and clawing at him but he clung on to his two friends and dragged them to safety. He said he'd never go back underground.

When Don Plunkett spoke folk listened.

'We know you want your gold back and to be fair that's understandable, but get this straight. The men who shot up Sailors Diggings will be punished. There ain't no deal with them, I done told you that already. Last I heard they killed seventeen. You don't pay nobody off just to get your gold back. We'll help you find the gold if we can. That reward you're offering should go to the families of the miners killed yesterday.'

Eddie Carter listened. This ain't going right, he thought, they think I'm one of the gang. If I ain't careful they'll like as string me up. Who can help me then? Well, Arnie for sure but he's back at the claim.

Then there's the drummer Quincy Roof, he patched me up and knows I'm not involved. If I can find him, they'll have to listen to him but I don't know where he is. And when I think about it, maybe they never saw me over at O'Brien either when I shot Cooper and the others.

Carter looked out of the corner of his eyes at Mooney. Mooney sat and stared at the fire, the embers still burned but the top of the fire started to crumble to grey ash with a red glow under the blackened logs. Mooney kicked a couple of large branches on to the fire and the dry leaves flared for a moment. A gun cocked and Plunkett aimed his weapon at Mooney and said, 'The next time you move I'll kill you.'

Mooney shrugged his big shoulders but did not say anything, he just squatted on his haunches in front of the fire, looking into the flames with a smirk on his face and waited.

Carter gazed at Mooney and thought, what in the hell is he so pleased about and why the hell is he banking the fire up. Goddamn it, I bet he's buried the gold under the fire pit. That's it, that's why he risked a fire in the night and is keeping it burning. That's got to be it, there's too much dirt around the pit when I think on it. He's dug it deep and put the gold under stones with the fire on top, he learned that from us yesterday.

Carter was about to call over to Crick and tell him but he stopped himself.

No, that's no good, I can't say anything, he thought. If I'm right and the gold's there they'll all think I know because I'm in on it with Mooney. I'd best keep quiet for now and see how it plays out.

He looked up as Melvin Priddy spoke.

'I say we hang them both here and now. Hang them first then talk to them later.' He took a rope off his saddle and said, 'I think—'

Crick interrupted him. 'I don't pay you to think, Priddy. Don't be an idiot. We don't kill them until they give up the gold. We can make them talk if we need to. I have people who can do that.'

Priddy's face burned with embarrassment and humiliation. He clenched his teeth, a lump of cartilage flexed in his jaw as he bit down on his anger and mumbled, 'You don't ought to talk to me like that.'

Crick ignored him, puffed his cheeks and blew out his breath, cleaned out his ear with his finger and said, 'I'll tell you what though, thinking on it maybe there's something in that. We could hang this one,' he pointed with his chin at Carter, 'and that will show Mooney we mean business.'

Carter began to chew on his finger nail and said, 'I done told you, I ain't with Mooney. I don't rightly know what I can do to show you that.' He paused, and he pulled at his ear, then asked, 'Do any of you know Quincy Roof, a bald trader who runs a wagon in these parts?' He saw the giant with the wild beard, Don Plunkett, nod and he spoke directly to him. 'I met him yesterday morning at my claim in California after Mooney shot me and before they killed those folk in town, he bandaged me up and knows I was chasing Mooney.'

'Enough,' said Crick. 'Mooney, does this man ride with you?' They all turned towards him but Mooney stared at the fire, picked at his teeth with his finger nail and kept quiet. 'Right, that's good enough for me,' said Crick, 'let's hang him and get to it with Mooney.'

'Hold on,' said Plunkett. He raised a finger at Crick to quieten him down. 'We've got to be sure we got the right man before we go stretching his neck. We need to do this right. Let's just cool our heels.'

Crick still sat on his horse, his arms folded across his narrow chest and his face tight with anger.

'What the hell is it with you people? First off, you say don't do a deal, you just want to kill them. Now you're whining, saying not to kill him because he might not have done it. Look, most of those who get hanged deserve what they get and that's good enough for me. If we hang him and he ain't one of them, he won't be complaining, will he?'

Plunkett spoke with authority and patience.

'Mooney's going to die. I need to be sure about this other feller. I'm going to ride back to Sailors Diggings and ask around. I'll see if I can find Quincy Roof, we can trust him. Let's see what he has to say. Why don't you keep searching for your gold while I'm gone?' He pointed a big thick finger at Crick. 'I expect to see Mooney here and that young feller

Carter still alive when I get back. Then we talk about who we kill and when we do it.'

Plunkett's voice rang with a heavy, quiet command and it seemed plain that Crick did not like it but it was just as obvious he was not the man to cross someone as tough as Don Plunkett.

Crick sniffed, looked away and said, 'Priddy, you stay here. I'll get as many as I can out looking for the gold. Now that it's got light we'll check the back trail from Sailors Diggings. When we've done that we'll come back and search that wood and those hills.' He pointed at Priddy. 'You wait here and you watch those two, you kill them if they move.' He rummaged in a saddle-bag. 'Here's some handcuffs, chain the two of them together, we'll cover you before we move out. We'll take all of the mules and horses except yours. We'll come back here in about two hours, I'll keep the screw key for the cuffs.' They took the heavy manacles and locked one of the metal rings around Mooney's right wrist and the other around Carter's left.

Crick looked at Plunkett. 'If you're not back with some news soon I'll kill the Californian called Carter.'

Carter closed his eyes and shook his head.

The others left, Priddy sat on a rock with a carbine laid across his thigh. Mooney looked at the flames and said, 'I'm keeping the fire going, friend, but I won't move from here.' As he spoke he glanced up, looked at Priddy and his eyes said, I'll kill you.

12

Mooney leaned forward and whispered to Carter, 'If you hadn't walloped me, I might have set them straight about you not working with me but you've got yourself in a fine pickle now and you won't get no help from me. Like as not they're going to hang us both come the afternoon, so I aim to bust out of here. Seeing as how we're chained together like a couple of wagon horses, you're coming with me, you hear me on that? Stay here and you die.'

Carter looked as mean as a bull whip but knew he was trapped. Mooney's right, he thought, there's a good chance they'll hang me unless Plunkett finds the trader Quincy Roof. Plunkett seemed a decent sort, I can maybe count on him. The rest look as though they might just string me up for the hell of it, I cain't take that chance. It's just like the dadburned war, I cain't sit back and depend on others, I can only rely on myself. I've got to get away from here first. Then I'll kill Mooney and set things straight.

His heart started to race, he tightened his damp hands into fists and whispered out of the side of his mouth to Mooney, 'I'll come with you but don't take that the wrong way, it ain't over between us.'

Mooney looked off into the sunlight across the fields and finally stared across the fire and said, 'Hey, mister.' Priddy glanced up. 'How would you like to make $30,000? I'll give you half of the gold if you let me go, we can ride out together. We can be long gone by the time the others get back. Thirty thousand dollars worth of gold, imagine what you could do with that and you can have it in the next ten minutes.'

Melvin Priddy was not a bad man. He didn't think too much about things, stuff happened and he didn't study on it. He drifted into a job with Crick who treated him like something on the end of a dung fork. He did the dirty work and got sassed by everybody. He accepted it, after all, that's how life had always treated him, even when he was young. He didn't remember his mother. Everyone called his pa Canada Bill, no-one said why but he'd never been anywhere near Canada as far as Priddy knew. Anyway, one day Canada Bill left him with a cousin and went up north panning for gold. Priddy watched him walk off in the rain. He never came back but then Priddy never thought he would. He left the cousin when he was fifteen or so and doubted anyone missed him. He drifted along for years then attached himself to Crick, someone who pushed him around and paid him not to think. He never expected anything and that's what he usually got. Until now, he decided, today was his lucky day. Thirty thousand there for the taking. He felt his time had come around and all of those folk who had used him, well, he was about to spit in their eyes. He did not hesitate.

'Yes, for thirty thousand you got a deal,' he said to Mooney. 'I'll let you go for that sort of money.'

Carter did not say anything, he sat with his head down and traced a circle in the dirt with the toe of his boot. How can you be so stupid, he thought, why would you trust a man like Mooney. I wish someone could explain that to me. He's a murderer and a thief. It's obvious that as soon as he gets the chance he'll kill you. But I cain't say anything, I need to get away and it looks like I'm stuck with Mooney for the time being. They took the key to the chains with them when they rode out so we have to go together but by God I'll see he dies for what he's done to me.

When they threatened to hang him, he felt terrified and the fear still clung to him like an old cobweb that he could not shake off. Anger welled up inside him, burned through him and lit up his cheeks but he took a deep breath and closed his eyes.

'Can you get these chains off us, mister?' said Mooney in a quiet voice.

'Nope, Crick's got the only key. Besides which, you're easier to handle chained together.'

'Sure thing, you're in charge right enough. I'm going to stand,' said Mooney. 'Don't get all riled up when I do. You're a rich man now, all you got to do is help us get out of here and I'll see you get what's coming to you.'

Carter sighed but kept quiet.

'Where's the gold?' said Priddy.

'Now take it easy, I ain't going to tell a smart feller like you straight off or you might get ideas about keeping the whole lot,' said Mooney. His eyes did not stray or blink as they locked on Priddy's face and stayed there. Mooney stood and yanked at the chain on his wrist, bringing Carter to his feet.

'Let's walk down the hill a piece,' Mooney said, pointing behind Priddy with his chin. The sky was bright blue and the land brilliant with sunshine.

'You see that twisted tree behind you in that stand of pine? Well, we need to start off from there.'

Priddy motioned for them to follow him, as they walked down to the tree they closed in a little on Priddy but Mooney did not hurry. Carter felt tense, he moved woodenly and because he waited for something to happen it seemed to take forever.

'You see that ridge?' said Mooney, pointing.

Priddy stopped and looked up and Mooney shifted alongside him. Mooney moved quickly for a big man; he locked his free arm around Priddy's throat and pulled him into his shoulder. Priddy's jaw went slack and his mouth dropped open. Mooney held him so tightly that Priddy could feel Mooney's breath on his cheek and smell the wood smoke in his clothes. He worked his mouth and tried to speak but in a harsh whisper Mooney said, 'You're going to hell, partner, and you ain't got the time for talking.'

Priddy sucked air in loudly through his mouth and then his breathing became more ragged as Mooney squeezed the life out of him. His eyes rolled back in his head and his legs buckled under him.

'Enough,' said Carter, grabbing the carbine out of Priddy's limp hand and pointing it at Mooney.

Mooney kept the pressure on, looked at Carter with contempt and said, 'Give me the gun right now or I'll snap his neck. Look in my eyes and tell me I'm lying.'

'I'll give you the gun but you leave that man be. We tie him up and get gone down the road, they'll be back in a couple of hours. If you kill him you'll have to shoot me and that shot will bring the others running. Then you'll have to drag me behind you when you try to make a run for it, you hear?'

Mooney took the rifle, kicked Priddy in the head and left him unconscious on the ground.

'Come on,' he said, 'let's go. There'll be a reckoning between the two of us right soon.'

Carter stood and looked at him and said, 'I'll be waiting at the end of the street for you whenever you want to come a-calling.'

Priddy was out cold, they left him tied up by the fire and rode out, doubled up, on his horse. Mooney rode behind Carter with the gun. They walked the horse for a couple of miles as the trail climbed upwards, slowly at first, cutting into the slope but it narrowed and curved high into the hills then sliced through the trees. The woods made heavy going, a maze of juniper, the floor a tangled carpet of briar and weed. Then the breeze smelled of water and they rode down a long sloping valley that fanned out into a bluff above a slow moving silent river. They did not speak, they had nothing to say to each other until finally Carter broke the silence.

'Ride in the shallows down river for a while then cut up one of the creeks on the far side and hope we lose them.'

Mooney grunted, he knew that he could not kill Carter while he was chained to him but he was impatient to be free and ride back to the camp and pick up the gold. He reckoned that it was unlikely that anyone would find the gold buried under the fire, they would just leave the camp and cover the fire. He could ride in after dark and pick the gold up but still he felt uneasy leaving it behind.

An hour later they left the river and rode up a shale wash, the earth broken and stony under a harsh sun. They passed up a long ribbon of water through a funnel of trees. Inside the trees the hot motionless air, bladed with sunlight and thick with flies, hit them like a fist.

Below them a track wound into a bank of hills and they saw an isolated dust-blown paintless frame house tucked against crag. The house shaded down one side by a screen of bitter cherry trees. The cabin looked still and dark like someone had died there and the place still mourned for them. Away from the cabin, a big boned mule that looked like it had seen a lot of miles, stood cropping nettles, his tail flicked lazily while he fed. The whole scene held a peculiar heavy quietness, a sense that something was not quite right about the place. They watched a tall figure splitting firewood on a stump by the barn, he placed a block of lumber on its end, hefted a range axe in both hands and split it in half with a dry thunk. He threw the kindling onto a pile, picked another hunk of wood and swung the axe again, absorbed in the work.

Mooney whispered, 'We'll ride in and get that farm boy to break this bracelet with the axe. Keep your arm down until I'm close enough to shove the rifle in his face. I won't kill him, don't fret none. We need him to swing that axe.' He dug his boots into the horse's sides and moved down to the cabin.

I've got to be careful now, thought Carter, Mooney will be holding the rifle and as soon as the chain is cut he'll be looking to shoot me and the farmer. He just wants rid of us so that he can ride back, sneak in and get the gold. I cain't warn the farmer though I figure Mooney could just as soon kill us both now and free himself. I'll have to hope that he don't realize that. I'll not say a thing, I'll play along until the chain's split. What the hell I do then I don't know, I hope I reckon on something right soon.

The farmer heard the horse walking down the slope as the hoofs thudded softly on a carpet of dust and he watched them in. As they neared he saw that the first rider was clean shaved with a good-natured face and no sign of a gun. The one behind him was a different matter altogether, he had a big body that looked like it was carved out of hardwood and a face straight out of a nightmare. His size seemed to give off a sense of uncontrolled violence and his face screamed get out of my way, I'm going to hell and taking you with me. The farmer twisted around and reached for his gun.

'Don't do it or you'll wake up dead,' said Mooney, his voice rasping like a rusty wheel.

The farmer stopped immediately and stood still. He wore a washed out threadbare blue shirt, the armpits dark with sweat, and a battered hat that looked like it had been trampled in a buffalo stampede and lank hair that shone with sweat. His neck was ringed with dirt and his skin so dark he looked like he had spent time smouldering on a bonfire.

'Take it easy, partner,' the farmer said. 'I don't got nothing worth stealing.'

'I can see that for myself,' said Mooney, pointing his rifle at the man's skinny chest. 'All I want is for you to bust this chain with that axe of yours.' He held up his arm and shook the manacles. 'Try anything and you got yourself a heap of trouble.'

'Step down then, boys,' the farmer said and he held the axe shaft across his shoulder. His voice cracked as he spoke, it sounded as though someone had their hands wrapped around his throat.

'My voice is a bit out of practice,' he said through a cough. 'I don't see many folk so there's only the dog to talk to and we ain't speaking to each other at the moment.' A dog yelped somewhere out back.

Mooney said, 'I figure you've left your pancakes on the stove too long, you're plumb crazy, mister. I got a notion that dog has more sense than you.'

'He reckons he does and that's why we ain't talking.'

Carter and Mooney dismounted and Mooney said, 'You got something to eat?'

'Bean mush and I think some chitlins from last week, it's just about better than nothing I reckon.'

'For God's sake, will you just cut this goddamn chain?'

The farmer nodded towards the stump chopping block, Mooney and Carter knelt on either side of it and stretched the chain across the scarred wood. Mooney still held the rifle one handed and covered the farmer. The farmer stepped up to the block, spat on both hands and rubbed them together, his calluses making a dry clicking sound. He lifted the axe above his head.

Mooney stared up at him and said, 'Jesus H Christ, you smell like an old saddle blanket that's been ridden on a soreback horse for hundreds of miles in August.' He lifted the rifle higher. 'Cut the chain straight down the middle,' he said, 'or I'll put a bullet in your guts.'

The farmer rolled his shoulders, looked away to

hide a sly smile and then he turned back and swung the axe. The blade hit the chain and sliced through it. As the blade hit the stump, the farmer dragged the axe back up and across and smacked the flat of the axe head against Mooney's skull. As Mooney toppled over, the farmer reversed the swing and brought the axe blade back across the other way to chop into Carter's head or shoulders. Carter had already rolled away and the momentum from the sweep of the axe swing threw the farmer off balance and he stumbled on to his knees. Carter jumped to his feet, lashed out a foot and his boot caught the farmer on the shoulder and the axe spun away. He saw that Mooney still held the carbine and was trying to get up. Carter knew he had to get to the woods, the trees offered safety, and the only thing the gun in Mooney's hand offered was death. Carter grabbed the half-conscious farmer by the scruff of his neck and dragged him away from Mooney.

Carter backed away then turned on his heels and ran down the slope, the manacle still on his wrist, the cut chain whipped down his leg as he ran. He dragged the groggy farmer with him. He ran for the mule, threw the farmer across its back, grabbed a handful of mane and cracked his palm across the mule's bony rump and the mule took off down the slope, bouncing the farmer along. As Carter reached the woods, he heard Mooney's rifle boom and a bullet spanged off a rock behind them but they disappeared into the darkness of the trees, the shadows

13

Mooney looked down the slope but there was no sign of Carter. He did not feel too concerned, he thought that Carter would come looking for him again or he was yellow and had run off, either way he'd deal with him. He touched the side of his head and felt an egg-like lump where the axe had caught him. His head throbbed like a Paiute war drum. He winced at the heat and the glare from the bright sky, and he hunched his head into his big shoulders and moved towards the cabin.

He stepped up on to the veranda, the wood rotten and porous, flaking and grey with age. The weathered wooden door yawned open, he pushed it with his fingertips and the hinges gave a parched creak. He went inside, the air had a dense musty reek like an old soup of sweat, dirt, food and tobacco that rose to meet him in a sticky layer. The stench covered his face like a wet cloth and he felt as though someone had stuck their fingers down his throat. He stopped, rolled a cigarette, dragged a match across a wooden post and took the smoke deep into his lungs, held it there and then let it roll out slowly through his nose. Holding the cigarette in his lips, he looked around with the smoke hanging in the air like a veil around his face.

The dry floor planks were powdered with dust and he heard his weight creak on the boards as he moved. He crossed to the smoke blackened fireplace and took a minute to look around. He crushed the last of the cigarette in his fingers, opened his hand and let the draught from the open door wisp the pieces away.

He knelt down to open an old wooden box that lay on the hearth and under some papers and letters, he found a decent looking Colt Dragoon with plenty of powder, caps and lead ball that all looked in good order. Mooney carried the box to the table. An old letter headed *Army of the United States* caught his eye and he took it out, flattened it with the palm of his hand and saw a certificate of merit from the Mexican war for action in Sante Fe awarded to Private Garret Baird. Mooney glanced up and looked through the open door and down the empty hillside.

'You must have had some salt at one time, Baird, but I reckon you found out you hadn't left Hell behind you. It came a calling again today.'

He crumpled the paper and threw it into the empty fireplace. He sat with the gun barrel pointing upwards and rubbed the gun over with a small cloth.

He turned the cylinder with his fingers one chamber at a time, loading them with the gunpowder, adding the ball and working the lever to get them in tight before sealing them with fat. He turned the Colt and pushed in the percussion caps with his thumb and finally spun the cylinder and watched the caps tick by. He loaded all six chambers and locked the cylinder on the safety catch. He laid the gun flat on the table, looked across and saw the crusted mush in a blackened pan on the stove. He ate from the pan, using his hand like a shovel. He saw the chitlins piled in a mouldy heap – they lay in enough fat to grease a wagon axle – and decided he wasn't that hungry.

He belched, jammed the gun down the waistband of his trousers and said to the empty cabin, 'Not a bad couple of days all in all. I'll have a few hours of sleep and then it's time to collect my gold and get gone.'

Down the valley, Carter ran as best he could by the side of the swaybacked mule. The mule's heavy laboured breathing whistled like the wind in a clogged chimney. He held the farmer belly down across the mule's withers.

I'll keep going, he thought, Mooney still has the horse and I'll reckon on him having at least the carbine. I can ignore him for a while and make my way back to his last camp. I'm sure the gold's there so that's where Mooney's going. Bet on it. That means if I wait he'll come to me and I can ambush him when he shows up. Let's hope those vigilantes have moved on. I'll have to be careful though, they still think I was with Mooney and I don't want to bump into them again, not without Mooney's dead body anyway.

The farmer stirred and Carter pulled the mule up and slid the man on to the ground. He knelt beside him.

'Are you feeling good enough to walk?' he said. 'The feller you clocked on the head with the axe will like as whale the life out of you if he gets hold of you.'

The farmer sat up and shook his head.

'I'll be fine, just give me a minute.' He looked at Carter. 'How in tarnation did I get here?'

'Well, when you hit him and tried to part my hair with your axe, I kicked you to quieten you down but I pulled you out of there. If I left you then Mooney would kill you for the hell of it.'

'I'm Garret Baird. Listen, I'm sorry I swung at you with the axe but the way I saw it, the two of you looked set on killing me. That Mooney has a face from hell.'

'He's got the face he deserves, I reckon,' said Carter, 'and I don't blame you for what you did. Out here you got nobody to rely on but yourself. I'd have done the same. I'm Edwin Carter, Eddie to my friends.'

They shook hands. Carter studied Baird, he had a worn face with leathery skin cobwebbed with wrinkles but his voice had changed since they left the cabin. Now Baird talked in a quick voice out of the side of his mouth and he seemed more alert.

'You've changed some,' said Carter, watching Baird's face. 'Back there you acted like you couldn't teach a hen to cluck.'

Baird looked at him then his gaze slipped away.

'I try not to show too much sense in front of strangers that are chained together and pointing a gun at me, especially when one of them looks like he was born and bred in hell, if you get my drift. Mind you, I ain't saying it's easy out here; loneliness ain't something that I can get used to. Sometimes it's like looking at the world from underwater. I cain't hear nothing and when the heat bounces off the skyline, the land's hazy and empty.'

Carter sensed that Baird was a fragile man who might snap if someone pushed him too far. His face had an unhealthy shine and hardness as if it was made out of glass and might shatter at any time. He glanced at Baird, who sat with his eyes fixed on him, waiting. Carter shrugged his shoulders.

'I reckon you're right there, friend, sometimes being alone feels good but other times this big land can crush you when you're on your own too much, especially if you've lost someone.' He looked at Baird but Baird avoided his eyes. 'I guess you can go back to the cabin in a couple of hours. Mooney will have moved on by then. Or you can come with me. We can just ride on a piece, I know which way Mooney will be heading and I aim to be there. He killed my partner and I've got to square things off with him, after that he won't bother you no more.'

'I'll come with you, Eddie,' Baird said immediately. 'That mule's game enough but he don't have much left in him, we'll have to take turns riding.'

They set off with the frail Baird moving like a man walking into a strong headwind.

Later they crossed the Illinois River, the banks lined solid with trees, everything cool and quiet in the thick shade. The mule struggled out of the water, straining for air as though his chest was wrapped in chains and his lungs made from wet paper. He snorted and tossed his head then, as his hoofs scraped on the wet stones by the cut bank, the mule stumbled and Carter rolled off him into the shallows. He stood, unhurt, with his clothes drenched through and moulded to his body, his hat brim pulled down and stringed with water cascading across his face. Baird hauled on the mule's reins, trying to get it to its feet.

Carter wiped his arm across his eyes and shook his head.

'Drop your gun,' said a quiet voice and the casualness in the tone made it all the more threatening.

Carter glanced up from under the sagging brim of his hat and saw a man he did not recognize, although he knew the type. A nameless man with blank hard eyes, a grim thin mouth and a holster low on the hip, the sort of face that had been hired to kill people for hundreds of years. He stood on a path speckled with sunlight.

'I won't say it again,' said the gunslinger. He drew a pace closer, his red-rimmed eyes locked on Carter and his thin face darkened by a two day stubble.

Carter held his arms out and said, 'We're both unarmed, no guns.'

'Hear me good on this, you two boys come out of the water and walk up the path, don't stop or look back. I'll be five paces behind you so there's no point trying anything. You've more chance of catching a weasel asleep than jumping me. We'll come back for that mule, maybe if we get hungry. Don't talk, no darn questions, there's a feller through the trees waiting for you.'

They walked up the grade through the woods and emerged into a sunlight clearing where Horace Crick, the owner of the assay office in Sailors Diggings, and another man sat on horses waiting for them.

Crick did not look good, the thought of losing the money still weighed heavily on him, he looked like a man nursing a permanent hangover. His big sweaty face had an oily sheen on his forehead and cheeks and a raw looking rash on his throat. He seemed a shiny podgy wreck of man.

'Yes, he's one of them, I thought it was him crossing the river,' he said. He sat on a roan horse with a scattergun tucked under his arm although he did not look as though he knew how to handle it. He stared at Carter and added, 'I knowed you'd be back. You're here to collect my gold, aren't you?

Where in tarnation did you bury it? It's well hidden, I'll give you that, we looked everywhere hereabouts. Look, I'm a reasonable man, listen good, the only folk here work for me. I don't give a goddamn cuss how many townsfolk you killed. Give me my gold and we'll let you be. You have my word on that.'

Carter felt the danger that surrounded him like a hand on his throat. The two men with Crick looked like sinister dark shadows on a lonely night ride and he knew that Crick's word meant absolutely nothing. He tried to look calm, he stood with a particular stillness and he spoke in a soft voice so that they all listened.

'I done told you already. I am not with the Mooneys. I did not kill anyone in Sailors Diggings and, for the fiftieth goddamn time, I did not steal your gold.'

His voice sounded hollow in his own ears. He felt the rage well up in a sudden tide, filling his whole body but he fought to stay relaxed.

Crick was not listening, his voice just hammered on.

'I've had enough of the likes of you. I ain't got no patience to waste on your sort. You need to know that killing folk is my line of work. It's part of my business and I think I got the market on it around here. I'll make you talk.'

He turned, holding on to the pommel and looked at the man sat next to him.

'Packett, do what you're good at, get to it. Set up a

fire and heat up your knife.'

Hillard Packett was a scrawny little man, all gristle and spit, the skin on his face looked a size too big for his head and hung pouchy and slack on his cheeks and neck. He had cold murderer's eyes that stared out of deep dark sockets as if he was figuring out how soon you'd beg for mercy.

He started a small fire, Crick turned back to Carter.

'Who's your friend?' he said, nodding at Baird.

'He's got no part in this,' said Carter, 'let him be. Mooney forced him to cut the chain,' he held up his wrist, 'and me and him ran for it before Mooney could kill us.'

'It's true, mister. My name's Garrett Baird, I live on the other side of the river maybe twenty miles south of here. I don't rightly know what's going on here but this feller,' he pointed at Carter, 'ain't no friend of that the other one called Mooney. We both had to make a run for it.'

Crick took his hat off and wiped his forehead with the sleeve of his jacket. He had a few strands of hair flattened with oil across his bald head, which looked polished and slick. He brushed a hand across his sparse hair as if he was checking it was still there then he wiped his palm down his trousers. He ran his thumb and finger down his moustache.

'See, this is what annoys the heck out of me, we get some dumb cracker like our friend Baird here who thinks he can interfere in my business when he don't know what the hell is going on. Well, let me tell you, Mr Baird, your opinion ain't worth the breath you drew to make it.' He turned to Packett who knelt by the fire holding a knife in the flames and said, 'Are you ready?'

Packett nodded and his knees cracked as he stood up. He was as gnarled as an old mesquite tree. He stared at Carter with a blank face and a cigarette jammed between his thin lips, his head curled into his thin shoulders. His hooded eyes glittered as he slithered across to Carter. He stopped and lifted the knife in his knobbly hand.

Crick said, 'Packett here likes hurting people, you need to know that. I reckon if he puts one of your eyes out you'll talk. That hot knife will slide through your eyeball like hot butter. Look, I'm a fair man, if you still say you weren't in with Mooney after we take one eye out then I'll probably believe you.'

'Now hold on there,' said Baird, 'you don't ought to do something like that. You ain't human, mister.'

He took a step towards Crick, whose horse lurched sideways a couple of steps. Crick looked over Baird and Carter and nodded and the gunman behind them stepped forward, whipped his gun hard across the back of Baird's head and said, 'He stinks like a scared skunk, pity I cain't knock the smell out of him as well.'

Crick pointed his scattergun at Carter and said, 'On your knees. Mess about and we'll kill your friend Baird first.'

Carter would not let that happen and they knew it. He knelt, the gunman wrenched his arm with the handcuff still on it behind his back, the cuff biting into his wrist. He roped Carter's arms, tied them back and knocked his hat off. Packett put a foot on Carter's chest and pushed him over. He knelt on Carter's shoulders and pinned him to the ground. Carter looked up as Packett and his knife moved in.

Hillard Packett was a strange man. He came from a decent family. His ma was a real nice woman. Hillard and his brother were mischievous when they were boys, they'd like as turn a racoon loose in a church service and such but, heck, most folk have done that. His brother turned out all right, he worked as a barber in Maryville, not the shop on the corner there but the one further down between the hardware store and the bath-house. Why Hillard turned out bad is anyone's guess. Maybe someone gave him a whaling or laughed at him when he was young and he never got over it. Maybe he just got in with a bad crowd. Maybe he was the bad crowd. No-one knows. But there was nothing in his background that could explain why he turned out wrong, why he cursed the day he was born and took it out on as many folk as he could.

Packett's eyes glistened with excitement and his cheeks burned with pleasure, his breathing quickened. Rasping like a blunt saw as he stared at Carter, he said, 'That's a hell of a feeling, ain't it, that's raw fear. I reckon a day ain't worth living unless it feels

14

'Stop right there,' said a voice. Carter realized he was holding his breath and he sighed and opened his eyes and took a deep lungful of air. He smelled pine, sweat and wood smoke and thought it had never smelled better.

Packett hesitated, the knife shuddered in his hand and he edged the blade closer to Carter's cheek.

'I'm warning you, mister, if that knife moves as much as a fly stuck in mud, I'll put a piece of hot lead through your thick skull, now back off right quick or you got yourself a whole mess of grief.'

They all looked around, a man stood in the gloom of a long green-black corridor of trees. He moved forward across ground matted with a thick layer of tangled grass and striped with shadow. The undergrowth rippled in the breeze and out strode Don Plunkett. He held a carbine, he looked as solid as the trees around him, as hard and unyielding as oak.

Crick looked livid, his face screwed up in a knot, as

red and hot as a well timed slap.

'Plunkett, what the hell are you doing here and what gives you the right to interfere in my business?'

'I'm here because that feller on the ground is telling the truth, he ain't with Mooney and never was.'

'Says who?'

'I do,' said another voice. Quincy Roof stepped out of the shade at the other side of the glade nursing a rifle in his hands, the breeze ruffling his beard. 'You know me, Crick, I've been trading in these parts for a year or two now. I saw that young man yesterday morning. He was wounded and set out to hunt Mooney, they'd just shot his partner. I was in his camp at Patrick Creek right after it happened. We sat by my wagon and I bandaged his side and fed him before he moved on.'

'Not only that, and hear me good,' said Plunkett, 'I talked to a couple of men who said they saw a feller in a blue coat and tan trousers like him up at O'Brien and we ain't seen him since. They reckon he killed at least two of the Mooney gang. Now back off and get gone before I lose my temper. I heard what you said about not caring who was killed. As I recall, that's the second time you've said something like that. Now you've got on my wrong side and I don't want to see your miserable face out here anymore today. Get your sorry hide out of my sight and take your men with you.'

The gunman cut the rope holding Carter and

Carter stood, walked over to Crick's horse and looked up at him. He did not speak, he held out his arm with the handcuff and chain and shook it quietly under Crick's nose. Crick undid the cuff and Carter let it thud into the dust and he stood and clenched and unclenched his hand.

His eyes rested thoughtfully on Crick for a moment and then he reached out, pulled Crick from his saddle and dragged him to the ground. Crick hit the floor like mud off a shovel. Carter grabbed the front of his coat and pulled him back to his feet. He raised his right hand, tightened his fist and held it like a lump of rock under Crick's nose, his arm muscles bunched as tight as iron when he drew back his arm. He hammered his fist into Crick's face, splitting his lips against his teeth. The punch brought tears to Crick's eyes and sent a tremor through his whole body. Blood from his smashed mouth stained his gums and teeth pink and a red froth dribbled across his chin. Crick threw his hands to his face and held his mouth, his eyes wide with fear then he dropped his hands to his sides and he stared at Carter with his bloodied lips pressed together.

'Come on, I'm going to lick you good,' said Carter, the skin on his face as white and stiff as candle wax. He stepped in close and his shadow fell across Crick's ruined face. Crick quivered like a leaf in a breeze.

'Please leave me alone,' he said, his voice little more than a cringing whisper.

'You'd like as kill a man before you'd made any

effort to find out if he told the truth. I won't forget that. It'll work out different next time round for me and you.' As Carter spoke, he pointed his finger with his thumb up like a gun and pretended to pull a trigger. 'Now get to hell and gone down the trail.'

Crick slid down the side of his horse and sat on the floor.

Hillard Packett edged across to his own horse without speaking. Carter's body seemed to hum with energy, he swung round with his right arm bent and his elbow out and caught Packett across the top of the nose. The bone shattered with a crack like someone cocking a rifle. Blood whipped from his nose across his cheek in long bright threads, leaving his face meshed in red.

'You're lucky you didn't touch me with that knife, mister,' Carter said. 'You'll get the death you deserve and I don't reckon it'll be a long time in coming.'

Packett wiped a smear of blood off his nose with his wrist, pinched the bridge of his nose with his fingers and said, 'We've all got to die some time. I'm going to make sure I deserve it when my time comes.' He struggled onto his horse, wheeled it around and rode out of the clearing back to Sailors Diggings.

Don Plunkett picked up Crick's hat from the ground, dusted it on his leg and rammed it down hard onto Crick's head. He bent, wrapped his arms around Crick like he was trying to lift a sack full of fat and hoisted him up, sat him on his horse and slapped a hand across its rump. Crick slumped in the saddle, hanging onto the saddle horn. He looked like he had been kicked from one end of Rogue River to the other as he disappeared up the trail after Packett. They all turned and looked at Crick's hired gunman, who stood in silence with Quincy Roof's carbine pointed at his back. Carter walked across and stood in front of him, he stepped up close, pointed a finger in his face and said, 'You got anything smart to say?'

'Don't be pointing your finger in my face,' said the gunman. He had a Colt in a rig on his right hip and another gun wedged down his waistband; his hand tightened on the gun butt in his rig.

Carter's shoulders relaxed but then his hand flashed out and he gripped the revolver in the gunman's waistband and drew the hammer back, they all heard the trigger sear lock into place. Carter said, 'Draw that gun and I'll pull the trigger and geld you like a horse, you'll be picking your nuts out of the dirt.'

The gunman sighed and said, 'I reckon you can leave me alone and let me find my own way to hell, don't you?' He nodded at Carter. 'You're as mean as a Mojave Desert wind but I ain't no pushover myself. Maybe we'll meet again further down the line.'

Carter looked at the floor, waiting for his anger to go and for his feelings to sort themselves out. After a moment or two he said, 'Get out of here.'

The man put a finger to the brim of his hat and sauntered off as if he was out for a stroll, they watched him ride off. Carter stood deep in thought, his eyes scanned the tree line and the spangled shade around the edge of the glade.

'Who else is in the trees?' he said.

Plunkett smiled and said, 'He's with us, Milton Shine, you can trust him. He'll make sure they don't double back while we sort ourselves out.' He held a hand out. 'I'm Don Plunkett.'

'Eddie Carter.' They shook hands. Carter looked down as Baird struggled to a sitting position. 'The feller on the floor with a sore head is Garrett Baird, he's a friend.'

Baird looked up, the pain in his head forgotten as he smiled his thanks at Carter.

'I hope you remember me from yesterday morning, son,' said Quincy Roof as he stepped forward. 'Them foil cartridges work out fine, did they?'

'Well, I'm still alive. They did, Quincy. I appreciate you speaking up for me, you sure got my acorns out of the fire on that one.'

'I reckon you ain't an easy man to kill anyway but I'm glad to help. We got someone else to see you as well, young Floyd from the livery rode out in my wagon with his grandpa, we left them back up the trail a piece. He's here to tell folk what you found out at the livery and how you figured out Mooney hid the gold. It all shows you're in the clear.'

Plunkett said, 'I doubt you'll ever convince Crick you didn't steal his gold, he doesn't trust anyone where his money's concerned. That punch you gave him has been a long time coming. Listen, we got your guns and horse as well, they're waiting back at the camp where you and Mooney were this morning.' Plunkett stopped talking when he saw the sombre intense look on Carter's face. 'What's wrong?'

Carter felt like he had a stomach full of cactus, he wiped his lips on the back of his hand and said, 'Get the horses in, we'll have to double up. We need to pour it on riding back to that camp. Mooney's heading back that way. I'll tell you what it's all about when we see that the boy Floyd and his grandpa are safe.'

15

They rode hard for the camp, emerged from the shadows of the last long draw and let the horses thunder across the soft earth. As the bush gave way to a sparse line of trees, they saw the rocks and Quincy Roof's canvas covered wagon with the tongue up in the air and the mules grazing to the side. Everything looked peaceful, young Floyd watched them in, he stood with Carter's black Morgan horse. He rubbed the horse under the jaw, stroked the short hair down his face between the eyes then he smiled and waved when he saw Carter.

'Let's eat,' said Roof, then he turned to Baird behind him. 'Come on, Garrett, I've got some clothes you can have that will make you look a real thoroughbred.'

Baird glanced shyly at the others and walked after Roof to the covered wagon. While they waited, a tall, fair-haired man arrived.

Plunkett waved across at him and said to Carter, 'This here's Milton Shine.'

Shine was thirty years old with a mouth that always wanted to break into a grin and eyes that sparkled like icy water. He wore a black wool coat and black trousers tucked into cracked dusty boots. He walked with a limp, favouring his left leg.

He had been hurt three times before. The worst one, the one that made him hobble, happened in late 1846 when he ran through a blistering curtain of bullets to pick up a wounded friend at the Battle of San Pasqual. Earlier in the year, he caught one in the shoulder at Sacramento and still had the puckered mark where the lead ball struck. The last one was a scar on his forehead from when he fell down a flight of stairs in a drunken heap in the Hot as Harry saloon in Ellensburg – that's the one he tended to talk about the most.

'How do,' he said as he dismounted and stretched his back.

Carter returned the smile. He vaguely remembered Shine from the fight on the hill at O'Brien, and said, 'Glad to meet you. Let's talk later; right now can we bank that fire up while we collect more wood? We need to keep the fire burning good all night and tomorrow. That fire will bring Mooney to us like a moth to a lamp. I'll explain while we eat. It's going to be dark soon.'

They all looked up and saw the light fading, the evening sky was streaked with purple and the dusk like a deep breath drifted in among the trees around them.

'Milton, could you set by the fire and keep an eye out for any movement on the hills or in the trees?' Carter said.

'Sure,' said Shine, 'I reckon I'm good at sitting.' He sat on a rock and laid his rifle across his thighs while the others settled in.

Later, with the kindling stowed and the food ready, they all hunkered down to eat. Quincy Roof and young Floyd carried plates piled with salted, battered pigs' feet, fried bread and corn fritters.

Roof said, 'Set by the fire and wade right in to what we got.'

They ate in a comfortable silence as the darkness fell around them.

'You look like a new man, Garrett,' Floyd's grandpa said through a mouthful of fritter.

Milton Shine nodded and said, 'He needs a bit of packing on them bones, I've seen more meat on the end of a fork. Mind you, he looks happier than a hog downwind of a full swill trough.'

Cleaned up Baird seemed a different man, he wore a chequered shirt with a button-down collar and blue flannel trousers cinched at the waist with a belt. His freshly shaved face looked fuller and his cheeks shone with colour.

'I feel good right enough,' said Baird, looking pleased. 'It's like I've just woken up for the first time in many a year.' He chewed on his food and said, 'I need to find my dog soon.' He looked over at Carter. 'He'll make my life hell if I don't share my luck with him.'

Both men smiled.

'What's your dog called?' said Floyd.

'He was my son's dog,' said Baird, and he looked down at his hands and coughed a dry dusty cough that seemed too heavy for his chest. He swallowed, suddenly tense and nervous as if he had just woken up and started talking about a nightmare that still scared him. He spoke quickly and his voice wavered at the final part.

'We called the dog Ulysses. See, in the Mexican war, I worked for a quartermaster officer called Ulysses Grant. I looked after the horses, did some blacksmithing and such but we was part of every battle, always up front in the thick of things. I liked Grant right well, he did his duty as good as any man I ever saw. He was about as nice a man as you could ever meet and I thought he was first rate.'

He massaged the back of his neck with the palm of his hand and felt embarrassed, he glanced around and saw that they all sat listening. He continued.

'I tell you something for nothing. At Molina Del Rey, a lot of men were hurt and Grant was the only officer I saw helping the wounded. He volunteered us for everything but did all right by me. He put me up for a certificate of merit. See, one day when we was out, I found a trail through dense chaparral and we sneaked in and took a Mexican battery. We defended that position for hours. I done all right, killed a few men, we turned the day and the Mexicans panicked and fled across the Rio Grande, a lot of them boys drowned.'

Carter handed Baird a small cigar. He lit it, closed his eyes and let the smoke drift out of his nose.

'I saw a lot of death and was just sickened by all those bodies on both sides laid out in the smoke of that war day after day. Piles of them mangled and coated in white dust like ghosts. I got mustered out in the end, spent a year living with the Lipan Apache, married a fine woman called Nashota and had a son called Kika.' He stared at the smoke drifting through his fingers from the cigar he held. 'They both died of fever first year we came up here.' He put the cigar in his mouth and looked up, his eyes half shut against the smoke from the cigar.

Everyone else sat with their gaze fixed on him, waiting for him to go on.

'After they died I just gave up on everything I guess, my boy would be about as old as that young feller,' he said, nodding at Floyd, his eyes swimming with tears. He pulled his hat down low, hiding his expression in the shadow of the hat brim.

After a moment Shine tried to lighten the mood and said, 'Anyone eating the last of that pork? I'm that hungry I could clean a whole hog down to the bones.' He speared the food with his knife and held it up. 'Me and hog meat go back a long ways. I was once drunk in Stevenson up off the Hood

River in Washington County, and when I stopped drinking I had a real live hog for company. I told everyone that I reckoned I'd won him in a card game. Next thing I know some farmer accuses me of thieving from his hog lot. He made more noise than a piano falling down stairs. Walloped me good, one minute I'm trying to explain and the next the floor came up and hit me hard in the face. Can you believe it, I was chased across a roof and out of town because of that hog. The farmer never caught me and I'm right glad, you wouldn't want to get on his wrong side.' He gnawed at the meat and smacked his lips.

'Did you really steal it?' said Floyd.

'Damn right I did,' said Shine.

'What's your story, sir?'

Shine shrugged his shoulders.

'Not much to tell I guess, I've been here and there, and done this and that. Reckon I'll move on soon enough.'

Plunkett looked up. 'Milt already gave up the money he had from panning gold to the families of the folks killed by Mooney.'

Shine said, 'Well, hell, I'd like have lost it at cards I guess, so it stopped me getting into bad company.'

'He ain't the only one neither,' said Plunkett. 'Quincy there gave a lot of his stock, like food, clothes and such to the families. It's all at their livery. We'll sort things out proper when we get back.'

'Least I could do,' said Roof, 'we all got to pull

together. I hope someone would do the same for my family.'

'We're getting help from others but some ain't interested,' said Plunkett. 'One in particular, that goddamn Horace Crick. He's sat in his big house making a fortune out of us placers but he won't help no-one but himself. I don't see that we should worry too much about helping him get his gold back. He can afford to lose it. He makes that much every durn month out of us placers. We're looking for justice for the folks they killed. Out here justice means killing all of them.' Plunkett thumped his fist in his hand and looked around. 'Don't it?' They all nodded. Plunkett turned to Carter. 'Eddie, you seem awful sure that Mooney's coming back here. Do you figure the gold's still in these parts?'

'Yes, Don, I do,' said Carter. He stretched his legs out towards the fire and threw his coffee grinds on the ground and watched them soak into the dirt. 'I reckon the best place to hide something is where everyone can see it. Like as not, the gold is buried under the fire right in front of us.'

They all glanced at the fire pit, the flames flickered and the dusk shadows danced across their faces. Carter sighed.

'When they killed my partner Nate yesterday, we had our bit of gold hid under the fire. I believe that Mooney remembered and used the same trick. Mind you, he needed a dadburned bigger pit.'

Garrett Baird glanced at Carter and said, 'Could

be, there's a heck of a lot of dirt piled around that pit, we didn't even dig them that deep in the Army. If you filled that hole there'd still be a whole lot of dirt left over.'

'Exactly, he'll have put the gold in and covered it with stones then built the fire over the top. Nobody looks under a fire.'

'It won't harm the gold, that's for sure.'

'Right. So, Don, he'll reckon when you don't find the gold you'll all move on and he can just ride in when it's quiet and pick it up.' Baird leaned forward, picked up a hunk of wood and poked it into the flames.

'Wait, Garrett,' said Carter. 'We keep that fire burning tonight. As long as there's a fire it tells Mooney we ain't figured out what he's done. It's all but dark, we wait for tomorrow. He'll be watching us right now.'

Grandpa spoke up. 'Ain't we sat like hogs in a pen waiting to be slaughtered?'

Plunkett tossed a branch onto the fire and smoke and ash drifted off into the dark.

'He'll wait, there's six of us so it's too risky and Eddie's right, all he has to do is hang around until everyone gives up and goes. Still and all, it's a mite uncomfortable letting him stalk us in the dark, makes your back itch, don't it?' He took his hat off and fanned the flames. 'Maybe the gold ain't here?'

'Maybe,' said Carter, 'but if it ain't we've only lost one night. Tomorrow some of us can turn the tables on him and hunt the hunter.'

Shine smiled. 'I guess it's like playing a blind hand at poker, we hope we've got four aces but it's his call tonight right enough.'

'Looks like we'll be digging that gold up twice over,' said Plunkett, 'but listen, it's a dangerous game and anyone who wants to leave can go. We won't think any the worse of you.'

No-one moved.

The trees surrendered quickly to the darkness, their trunks faded into black columns like rifle barrels and the leaves trembled beside them.

They sat drinking coffee. Grandpa pulled his pipe out of his vest pocket, scrapped the bowl with a knife then packed it with tobacco and lit it with a burning twig from the fire. Quincy Roof handed round cigars and chewing tobacco laced with molasses. Carter bit a lump out of a plug of tobacco and sat with his jaw packed. Plunkett chose a cigar, bit the end off, picked a piece of tobacco off his tongue and lit up. He leaned his head back and blew a plume of smoke into the air. It mingled with the smoke from the fire and curled upwards and broke apart in the breeze. The smell of tobacco and burning wood filled the air. They waited.

The moon came out for a short while and then big banked clouds rolled in from the west and the wind picked up. The dark clouds bunched and drifted like black smoke and then, pressed down by the leadened sky, they shrouded the tops of the trees. A fine spray of rain swept in, the canvas on the wagon slapped in the wind and it tugged their coats open and pushed at their hat brims.

'It looks like it's going to be a real frog-stringer for a while, don't it?' said Plunkett. 'Maybes we can use it as cover and have a look around.'

Carter stood up and stretched his back, it felt like a burning cord tightened around his hips.

'Let's do it,' he said. 'I need to ease my back anyways. I guess Mooney expects us to move around some. Me and Don will take a walk out yonder while the rest of you get some sleep under the wagon. Stow some lumber in the wagon out of the rain, we need it for the fire.'

Garrett Baird looked up and said, 'We'll bank it up and leave it burning like any other night.'

'I agree,' said Carter, 'you fellers sleep.' His face hardened. 'Nobody wears a hat tonight. If we see anyone wearing one we know it's Mooney.' He looked at Plunkett. 'Don, we'll split up and wander around some. We ain't looking for trouble in the dark.'

'No, but trouble usually comes whether you're looking for it or not. If we find it, we take it to Mooney good and proper.'

As they moved away, the wind clattered over the brow of the hill and the first hard drops of rain hammered on the canvas bonnet of the wagon like gunfire.

16

Carter was glad to get away from the others, he enjoyed their company but mostly he liked to be on his own. Tonight he wanted time to think, tomorrow the killing would begin. He moved through the trees and headed north towards a high ridge. The rain started but when he reached the top of the incline and looked back, the fire still burned and in its uncertain light he could see the wagon and a couple of mules silhouetted against the shadowed rocks.

He moved on, following the shoulder of a rise that climbed up before a pathway swept up the gradient and tapered into a muddy track that curved high over the hill. The rain swept in, driven by a bitter night wind and burst against him. He moved through a curtain of water that thrashed the trees. Even with the downpour, he began to sweat and the two day growth of whiskers that peppered his face and neck began to itch. As he breathed, the cold air felt like a razor on his throat. He gazed at the lines of trees as they drifted away from him in the dark.

All he could hear was the swish of his own footsteps in the drenched grass. His boots glossy with wetness, the rain water seeped through and dampened his feet.

The shadows changed as he moved and in his imagination, he saw Mooney standing in front of him, breaking and reforming in the shifting darkness. Carter felt his heart pound in his chest. He pictured Mooney waiting to draw him in and kill him. He lost the track in the blackness of the hills, he could not make anything out in the gloom but he remembered the lay of the land and went on.

Fear like a pain clenched his chest and twisted down into his stomach. He slid forward, waiting for the trees to come to him out of the shadows. Rain pelted down in the darkness, drummed on the leaves and splattered on the mud. His wet hair, plastered to his head, shone like it was oiled.

It reminded him of a recurring dream that haunted him when he was young where something, or someone, chased him through an endless forest. He just knew that danger lurked behind every tree but he ran on in panic and fear, unsure where he was going or where he had been. The memory came back to him now like the shot of a gun. Turn back, he thought, but he realized that it was just his mind playing tricks on him, he had no intention of going back. Fear only comes if you let it in, he reminded himself, he straightened his back and pressed on.

There was no give in him at all.

As suddenly as it started, the rain stopped and the clouds moved south, dimming the land. The moon poked out and dull chrome light silvered the trees and undergrowth. The wind blew a chain of cold raindrops off a branch and it ran over his face and pattered across his shoulders and back like buckshot. He knew where he was. He stood on a high butte, and he made sure there was no-one about and stole across to look down the sheer side with the river far below. The water shone like a sliver of ice in the silvery light. Beyond the river hung the shadow of the far hills and trees climbed the high ground into a black sky.

He doubled back and looked towards the other side with a clear view of the valley and camp site below. He noticed trampled undergrowth on the ground to his right and saw two cigarette butts in the grass. It looked like someone had stood for a time and studied the camp already. Mooney must be around.

Carter decided to get off the hill, he eased back into the thick blue-black shadows of the trees and worked his way back to camp. He took his time through the woods, passing down the incline until the ground levelled off. He stood and waited in the damp blanket of the night, stood in the smell of wet pine and rotten wood and the sound of the rain water ticking off the leaves as they shivered in the milky moonlight. His eyes searched the gloom for movement. As the wind eased, he left the protective murky darkness of the tree line and walked quickly across the open ground.

Just shy of the camp, he crawled under an outcrop of rock filled with the heavy scent of damp leaf mould, the wetness soaked his elbows and knees. He stretched out and dozed. After about half an hour he stirred and without really waking up, he saw Don Plunkett cross the camp and push his way under the bed of the wagon.

The next time he opened his eyes it was early dawn, he pulled himself out and stirred the fire into life. Weak flames fluttered in the frail grey light of a new day. He took wood from the wagon to bank up the fire and as he glanced down, he saw Don Plunkett watching him from the shadow of a wheel, holding a gun in his hand. When Plunkett realized it was Carter he smiled, stood and slid the gun into his waistband. They got the fire going and let the heat dry their damp clothes. The smell of coffee woke the others and they edged out, stretching and shaking themselves free of sleep. They started towards the fire but Carter held a hand up to stop them.

'Stay there,' he said. He studied the ground, skirted the fire pit with an animal alertness in his movements, hesitating a couple of times. He raised his eyes and looked off towards a small stand of pine and then, satisfied, he straightened up and motioned the others towards him and said, 'None of you came out to the fire in the night, did you?'

They shook their heads and Milton Shine said, 'I don't reckon any of us moved, all I could hear above the wind and rain was Quincy snoring like a hog with a cold, reminded me of a woman I once knowed in Medford.'

'I don't snore,' said Roof.

'Well,' said Shine, 'someone must have drove a herd of buffalo through here last night.'

Carter said, 'Mooney came in and looked around.'

Roof picked a scattergun out of the wagon and they watched him cock it and glance around. The gun shook in his hand.

'He's gone, Quincy, for now,' said Plunkett. 'Looks like you was right about the gold, partner,' he said, looking at Carter. 'I figure he was checking the gold was still there. That means he'll be back.'

Carter faced them across the fire pit.

'Look at me,' said Carter. 'Now don't make it obvious but there's a high butte over my right shoulder. The land rises up and the top's fringed with trees, I reckon he's there. I was up there last night and I'm pretty sure he watched us from the top. I'd guess that's where he is right now like as not, looking down like a hungry buzzard.'

'What are you going to do?' said young Floyd.

'Eat breakfast,' said Roof. He uncocked the gun and pushed it back in the wagon. 'I'll cook up something while you figure out what to do.'

'Come on, Floyd,' said his grandpa. 'Let's build that fire up and eat, a man can do most anything on a full stomach.'

'Yes, sir,' said Floyd, 'and me and Mr Baird will see to the horses.'

The others sat by the fire and smoked while Carter cleaned his Sharps carbine as best he could. He took time to wipe out the gunpowder residue from the breech, blew it clear with the lever down and the breech open then he set it aside and took out a Colt Navy. He checked the foil cartridges were all in place, spun the cylinder with the palm of his hand, set the safety and slid the gun into his rig. He checked a second gun and hefted it in his hand, enjoying the feel of the cold weight; he ran a thumb down the barrel and tucked the Colt down his waistband.

They ate chops with bread fried off in the fat. Plunkett gnawed the meat off a bone and tossed it onto the fire, the last of the fat flared brightly in the flames and he said, 'Garrett, you've been in the Army, right? We could sure use your help in Sailors Diggings, that's if you're minded to help out. I reckon with what you know from being a quarter-master you could organize food, clothes and such like for the families of those killed.'

Carter thought Baird might have doubts but he seemed to have grown in confidence in the last day because he looked up, grinned and said, 'That I will, Don. I'd be right glad to help out.'

Grandpa watched him while sucking the grease off his fingers. He wiped his mouth with his shirt sleeve and said, 'Listen, Garrett, me and Floyd have an idea of our own. We'd like you to come and work with us at the livery, you know, blacksmithing and such. You said you done that sort of work in the Army. I'm getting too old for the heavy iron work.'

'What does Floyd think?' said Baird, looking straight at the youngster. 'Are you for it?'

'You bet,' said Floyd. 'I reckon I can learn a heap of stuff from you.'

Grandpa said, 'The livery will be Floyd's when he's old enough to take it on proper but you can board at the stables to start with and we'll pay you what we can.'

'Money don't bother me none,' said Baird, 'but I'd be right glad to work for you and earn my keep. Things sure seem to be looking up for me.'

Above them on the butte, Mooney watched them in a deep deathly silence. He held a rifle in his hand and Baird's Colt tucked down his trousers.

17

'What about Mooney?' said Roof, gathering up the tin plates. 'What are we going to do?'

'Kill him,' said Plunkett. 'His life's been one long horse ride to hell. Let's get to it.' He clenched his right hand, the knuckles whitened and his fist looked like a sledgehammer. 'If you ask me we should go get him today, he came in last night and we cain't risk him doing that again. He might just take it into his head to start shooting, I don't like just sitting here with him out there.'

'I agree,' said Shine, 'we cain't just accept the hand we've been dealt. Let's take it to him hard and fast.'

Carter nodded and said, 'Milt, are you handy with that gun?'

'If it breathes I can kill it,' said Shine, laughing. ''Course I'm better if the other feller ain't got a gun and he's standing still and looking the other way.'

Carter scratched his head through his hat and

said, 'You know, that's given me an idea about getting Mooney to look the other way. What we do is start to break camp real slow and let him,' he nodded towards the ridge, 'think we're leaving. Milt wanders off into the trees over yonder where the trail goes behind those rocks and he kicks up a storm shooting and hollering. It's safer if you shoot into the tree trunks, Milt, then no-one catches a stray bullet. Some of us rush in after you and you keep the commotion going while me and Don make our way up the butte in the trees. Mooney will be too busy looking down here wondering what in tarnation is going on. We'll split up and move in on him from each side while he's trying to make out what the hell is happening.'

Plunkett stood up and clapped Carter on the shoulder and said, 'I like that a lot, we squeeze in and crush him while he's looking the other way.'

Shine stood and hitched his gun rig up on his hips and loosened his shoulders.

'Take it easy, Milt, them trees ain't going to shoot back,' Plunkett said.

Shine said, 'Those trees are as good as dead already.' Then he looked serious. 'When the shooting starts up there we'll come a-running, count on it.'

Carter turned to Roof. 'Quincy, if you feel it's going against us you get that youngster and his grandpa out of here, you hear me on that? Get down the trail to the settlement and bring some help out here right quick.'

Roof rubbed his chin with his fingers and said, 'I

will for sure but it don't seem right, us getting that gold back for Crick and it maybe costing some of our lives.'

Carter said, 'I've been studying on that myself some, if we get back we'll talk about it.' He took a deep draw on his cigar, tossed the butt on the dirt at his feet and ground it out with the toe of his boot. He let the smoke drift out of his nose and mouth as he said, 'Let's do it.'

'You'll be back,' said young Floyd. 'I know it.'

Roof handed Milt Shine two extra fully loaded Colt Dragoons.

'There's nothing special about them, Milt, but they're reliable, they take five rounds. Remember that and make them last.'

Shine stuck them down his waistband, pulled his trousers up but did not speak or try to make a joke; he just turned and walked off to the trees.

'I'll go up the right, Don, if that's fine with you?' said Carter.

'See you at the top,' said Plunkett.

They watched Shine disappear into the woods, the sun glowed and unblemished heat and light poured over them. The last they saw of Shine was his back netted in shadow from the canopy of pine trees and then he disappeared into the woods.

'Let's hitch up the team,' said Roof. 'We take our time and make out we're leaving.'

They worked in silence, the only noticeable sounds in the camp the jingle of the bridles, the horses stirring and the creak of the wagon as they loaded up. The smell of horse and mule mingled with the harsh tang of wood smoke, the fire gave a dull dusty sigh as the charred embers caved in on themselves and a cloud of white smoke curled up around their ankles. Even though they waited for Shine's first shot it took everyone by surprise when it came. The crack made the mules jump, snort and shake their heads, birds cawed in alarm and lifted from the trees until the sky was flecked with them as they spiralled away.

Shine shouted and the men turned and rushed into the timber towards him.

Carter ran, he saw Shine's shadowy silhouette wave to him as he passed but he did not stop or speak. He cut east and ran through the matted undergrowth and then his steps shortened as he started to move up the incline. He heard more shouting and another shot but did not look back. He shut everything else out, he could only hear his own heavy breathing and the thud of his own boots, he felt the thump of each step resonate through his body as he ran. Sweat trickled down his face and back like raindrops and his damp shirt clung to his back, the air layered with heat and dust clawed at his face.

No time for patience now, he thought, I'll just pour it on up here and ease off when I hit the clearing at the top. I need to get in close, if I shoot from too far away I might hit Don coming up the other way. He held an arm up to brush the bushes out of his way. I hope to God Don's careful when he opens up. Damn it, of course he'll watch out, he's no greenhorn, he'll do the right thing.

His doubts from the previous night suddenly lifted, he felt them disappear, his spirits picked up and he ran on full of energy and purpose, his muscles hard and corded like rope.

After a couple of hundred paces, his legs started to shake with fatigue and he looked up the grade, measuring the distance to the top. He could see the glare of the brittle sunlight through the trees where the ground levelled off and the timber opened up. He began to walk taking deep breaths, his face ran slick with sweat, he rubbed it with his hand and wiped his palm down his trouser leg. He drew one of the Colts. He edged his way through the brush, blinked a couple of times to let his eyes adjust to the brightness and waited. His gaze followed a sandy path and he saw footprints etched in the dirt. A cool wind pushed through the grass that hid him and leaves lifted and rustled above his head. The trees fluttered with shadow.

He looked out of the dark shade through gaps in the trees like gates of sunlight, and he studied the landscape and tried to picture in his mind where he went last night. Ahead on the right he remembered the clump of trees in a fold in the land where branches reached the ground like dark caves. He felt certain he skirted that in the night and came out by the rocks and trees where Mooney had stood, smoked and watched their camp.

Apart from the foot prints he found no other signs of Mooney but Carter guessed he would be in the same place. He heard another shot echo up from below and he started to move.

Then he had him. Hunkered down by a clump of rocks, he glimpsed Mooney's hat and burly shoulders by the trunk of a fallen tree, looking down the incline. Carter crept forward, lowered himself to the ground and inched his way across the thirty paces to a lichen-covered boulder where he knelt and glanced across to the deadfall. Mooney had gone.

Carter heard the three clicks of a gun being fully cocked and a shadow fell across him.

'Well, if it ain't my old partner,' said Mooney in a deep hoarse whisper. He stepped through fern and brush and stood over Carter, blocking out the sun like a huge thunder cloud.

'I just saw some big feller lumbering up the other way making more noise than a cattle drive and thought I'd go round and pick him off when I stumbled across you scuttling about like a skink in the grass.'

Carter threw himself forward and crashed into Mooney's legs. As he hit him, a pain from the wound in his back shot down his leg but Mooney toppled over backwards and Carter fell with him in a tangle of arms and legs. Mooney went down hard, his back crashed with a solid thump against the ground and whacked the air from his lungs in a whoosh. His gun flew from his hand and clattered into the rocks. Carter swept his own Colt up but a huge calloused hand clamped on his wrist and wrenched his arm aside. Mooney's grip bit into his arm like a vice twisting his elbow. Carter glanced down and saw Mooney glaring up at him with eyes filled with malice, his ruined face stiff and set like a death mask. Mooney levered his huge shoulders upwards and pushed Carter sideways like he weighed next to nothing. Mooney's left fist swept over and caught Carter on the temple, knocking his hat off and slamming his head into the dirt. Carter's gun hand lost all feeling under the pressure of Mooney's iron grip and he felt the Colt slip out of his fingers.

Carter brought a knee up and caught Mooney in the groin and the big man coughed, retched and let go of Carter as he lurched to his feet. He backed off a pace, doubled over with his hands between his legs.

'You'll pay for that, mister,' he gasped as Carter scrambled to his feet.

Carter swung a punch and felt his arm jar as he caught Mooney on the point of the chin, he grazed his knuckles and it felt like he had walloped a rock. Mooney's head did not move, he simply smiled a grimace as stiff as an iron bar and thrust forward, fastened his brawny arms around Carter's waist and pinned his arms to his sides. Mooney grunted and lifted Carter off the ground and squeezed. An excruciating pain from Carter's wound shot up his back, he gasped in anguish and his spine arched in fresh agony. Mooney cast him aside like an old coat. Carter tried to roll away but Mooney seized his shirt collar with one hand and grabbed his belt in the other and heaved. Carter felt himself lifted into the air. Mooney held him like a fence post across his chest and walked to the other side of the clearing where a sheer drop of fifty feet or more fell to the rocks and river below.

Mooney grunted, straightened his arms and jerked Carter above his head. Carter looked over his shoulder. He smelled the wet air, he saw the emptiness that plummeted down to glossy boulders webbed with moss by the edge of the water and the wide river that looked to have a solid black metal surface, far below.

'Time to die,' said Mooney.

'If I don't get you in this life I'll be waiting for you on the other side,' said Carter.

'See you in hell then. Tell them to bank those fires up, hell ain't hot enough for the likes of me.'

Mooney took a deep breath, swayed and let Carter fall.

But he did not go far. Carter collided with the ground immediately, he twisted and saw Don Plunkett holding Mooney. Plunkett had pulled him back from the edge and Mooney had dropped Carter onto the rocks just short of the fall into the river.

Mooney and Plunkett faced each other, they stood toe to toe and some primitive, instinctive challenge passed between them. They measured each other up.

Mooney was the taller of the two, his triangular back and his biceps bulged with power from the slabs of thick muscle across his chest and arms. Plunkett had a solid body, a neck as wide as his head, a barrel chest with a thick stomach to match and a back like a bull, forged from the heavy lifting and the daily hard labour in the mines of the West.

They moved around each other warily, Mooney shot out a hard right looking for Plunkett's chin but Plunkett slapped the blow aside and drove a pile driver like a jack hammer into Mooney's guts, snapping a rib.

'You'll have to do a whole lot better than that,' said Mooney but he wheezed as his voice outran his breath.

He smacked a fist into Plunkett's face and the chain from the handcuff whipped across and burst Plunkett's nose, throwing a mess of blood down his beard. Plunkett blinked and rolled forward, and he pummelled Mooney's body with a barrage of jolting blows. In desperation Mooney wrapped his arms around Plunkett's solid body and squeezed until the muscles in his arms stood out as thick and banded as wire cable. Plunkett simply head butted Mooney in the face, crunching his nose, then he swung both arms out wide and boxed his ears. Mooney coughed a deep harsh bark that ripped through his chest. His eyes glazed over and the energy and strength washed out of him. He tried to claw at Plunkett's eyes but a big roundhouse blow that he never saw coming caught Mooney on the hinge of the jaw by the ear, a humming noise filled his mind and he felt himself sink into a pit of mist. Mooney backed away blindly, swaying on the edge of the cliff, his legs seemed boneless. In panic he reached out and grabbed the front of Plunkett's shirt with the last of his ebbing strength. They stood locked together on the lip of the cliff like a couple of dancers in a last embrace. Mooney stumbled towards the sheer drop and dragged Plunkett with him.

Carter lay on the floor behind them, he scrambled forward on all fours and clutched Plunkett's legs and wrapped his arms around them and dragged him to a halt. Plunkett looked straight into Mooney's blazing eyes, pushed his thick arms upwards and broke Mooney's hold. He put a big hand over Mooney's face and pushed. Mooney stepped backwards into nothing, he screamed in terror and fell from sight, he cartwheeled down the sheer drop and crashed into the rocks below.

'Don, will you quit messing about with him, my back's hurting something awful,' said Carter. Plunkett smiled and hauled Carter to his feet.

They both leaned out and saw Mooney's body, laid like a puppet that someone had grown tired of and thrown into a corner. The river water lapped underneath him, making it look like his arms moved.

'We'd best go down and make sure he's dead,' said Carter.

To their astonishment, Mooney shook his head

and slowly struggled to a sitting position. Carter walked off, picked up Plunkett's rifle and strode back without speaking. He pulled the hammer back, tucked the stock up to his cheek, sighted down the barrel and squeezed the trigger and shot Mooney. Mooney fell back and his blood billowed and floated in the cold river like a red cloud.

'That's the last nail in his coffin,' Carter said.

'You're an unforgiving man, Eddie,' Plunkett said.

'He don't deserve any mercy, downright bad needs to be paid for somewhere down the line.'

'I'm with you on that, partner, I'm right glad we got it done. Mooney looks small and mean now he's dead, don't he?'

The two men stood side by side and gazed past the overhang and out across the sweep of land below them.

'You know, Eddie,' said Plunkett, watching the horizon, 'one mistake and either of us could be down there with him. Life sure feels good right now, don't it?'

'Ain't that the truth.' The two friends enjoyed the unblemished sunshine, the clear ceramic blue sky, the thickly wooded mountains and the tangled grass on jumbled hills crisped to a fine summer gold. The land at their feet burnished like a lake of sunshine. They heard footsteps and turned as Garrett Baird and Milton Shine came across the open ground towards them.

'It's settled then,' said Shine.

'It is,' said Carter. 'Mooney's dead at the bottom of the rock face down yonder.'

Shine did not bother to look, he turned and hobbled back to the camp to tell the others. Baird had collected Mooney's horse and led Carter and Plunkett down to the river to collect the body. They slung Mooney over the back of his horse and walked back to the camp in silence.

They packed up and prepared to leave. They took their time, cleared the fire away and brought out the gold. The bags were charred and burnt through in parts but they repacked them in a couple of spare burlap sacks.

Roof looked from the gold to Mooney's dead body and said, 'If he hadn't been greedy and come back for the money he might have got clean away.'

'No, sir,' said young Floyd. 'With Mr Carter and Mr Plunkett on his tail, it was always going to end this way.'

'Listen,' said Carter as they threw the last sack onto the wagon boards with a dusty thud. 'It would sure stick in my throat just to give this gold back to Crick. I talked it through with Don there,' he nodded across to Plunkett, 'and we'd like to hold on to it and share it out amongst the families of those killed by the Mooney gang.'

Plunkett nodded and said, 'See, Crick was willing to do a deal with Mooney, he was ready to pay him to get his gold back and let Mooney go. I don't hold with that. He won't help those folk that are suffering in the settlement. And don't forget, he'd've killed Eddie here without a second thought.'

'I'm for it,' said Grandpa, 'but there'll be a heap of trouble when Crick hears about it.'

'He won't hear it from us. We tell no-one. We stick together. Out here we're all we've got,' said Carter. 'Crick must never know.' He plucked at his ear lobe. 'Remember, we say nothing, not ever. We head back with the body and the story is we killed Mooney but we never found the gold. Hell, we tell them we never even looked for it, we just wanted Mooney dead. Crick can keep searching if he wants to.'

Plunkett sat back on the tailboard of the wagon and said, 'Here's how I see it working. Back at the settlement, me and Garrett will organize things so that the gold is sold off a bit at a time. It won't take too long. Crick's assay office sees plenty of colour through every week.' He hefted a sack of gold in the back of the wagon. 'There's thousands of placers working claims in these parts. We pretend to work the claims of the folk who got killed. We take gold from these sacks a bit at a time and say we panned it. The families take it to Crick's assay office and sell it to him. It would be a sight quicker if Milt would help out, we cain't tell no-one else.'

He glanced at Shine and raised his eyebrows.

'I ain't against it,' said Shine. 'Goddamn it, for a minute there I had over $75,000 in gold, I was richer than possum gravy.' He pretended to flick a coin in the air. 'And then I just agreed to give it away. It's a grand idea, boys, the families get help and Crick buys back his own gold. It's like a gift from Crick. I like that, I like that a lot.'

And that is exactly what they did. It worked out fine.

18

These days there's a plaque by the side of the trail that includes the following:

> *In 1852 English sailors jumped ship in Crescent City to go east in search of rumoured gold strikes and found colour here at what became known as Sailors Diggings. By 1856 this had become the town of Waldo, the first territorial seat of Josephine County. As the gold played out, many of the residents drifted away. The town was levelled by the giant hydraulic water cannons of the placer mines. The dreams of its residents now gone, only the occupants of the hilltop cemetery remain to watch over the once thriving community.*

Horace Crick is buried in that cemetery. The loss of the gold changed him, he was never the same again. He wasted a lot of money searching the land around

Sailors Diggings. He hired men to look for clues, caves, anything that would help him find his missing gold. They reckoned it sent him plumb crazy, in the end he used to walk the streets and mutter to himself. Folk never felt any sympathy for him though, there was still that something about him that people could not abide. He never found his gold of course. He would have been a whole lot crazier if he had known that he bought the missing gold back again when the families brought it into his assay office. The stolen gold ended up back in his strong room.

Young Floyd grew up and moved on, he went on to own three stables including a livery and horse corral out in Arizona Territory, in a place called Tombstone. He did right well out of it. The corral fronted Allen Street with a rear entrance lined with horse stalls on Fremont Street, he named it Old Kindersley after his grandpa but everyone just called it the OK Corral. You may have heard of it. There was a gunfight up that way one time.

Ulysses S. Grant remembered Garrett Baird and he sent for him during the Civil War. Baird worked for him throughout that bloody conflict and stood at the Appomattox Court House in April 1865 when the confederate Robert E. Lee surrendered to Grant as Union Commander. Baird mustered out as soon as he could and went back and worked for Floyd for the rest of his life.

Quincy Roof spent his summers trading through

Oregon and California for a couple more years. The good news was that the waster his daughter married turned out fine in the end; he knuckled down and made a decent job of helping Quincy run his store in Marysville.

Sad news about Don Plunkett though, after all the good work he did in Sailors Diggings. True to his word, he used all of the gold over the next year or so to see that the families of those killed were looked after properly. He moved on. A few years later, he worked the silver mines of the Comstock Lode in Nevada. A tunnel collapsed and Plunkett and two others went in to rescue the trapped miners. They sent six survivors to the surface but there was a second cave-in and Plunkett and the rest never came out.

Later, Carter heard that one of the men who went down with Plunkett was a cheerful feller with a limp, but he also heard that someone saw Milton Shine across the border in Canada, married with two children and farming in a place called Saltcoats. Carter hoped that was true.

When he heard about Don Plunkett's death it hit him hard, he went down there and laid a stone in the local graveyard even though they never found Plunkett's body. The inscription read:

You could do worse than have a friend like Don Plunkett.